# THE BOY WHO REVERSED HIMSELF

Other books by William Sleator

Singularity
Interstellar Pig
Fingers
The Green Futures of Tycho
Into the Dream
Among the Dolls
House of Stairs
Run
Blackbriar

# THE BOY WHO
# REVERSED HIMSELF

## WILLIAM SLEATOR

E. P. Dutton    New York

*Library of Congress Cataloging in Publication Data*

Sleator, William.
  The boy who reversed himself.

  Summary: When Laura discovers that the unpopular
boy living next door to her has the ability to go
into the fourth dimension, she makes the dangerous
decision to accompany him on his journeys there.
  [1. Science fiction]  I. Title.
PZ7.S6313Bo  1986  [Fic]  86–19700
ISBN 0–525–44276–6

Published in the United States by E. P. Dutton,
2 Park Avenue, New York, N.Y. 10016,
a division of NAL Penguin Inc.

Published simultaneously in Canada by
Fitzhenry & Whiteside Limited, Toronto

Editor: Ann Durell    Designer: Isabel Warren-Lynch

Printed in the U.S.A.   COBE   First Edition
10 9 8 7 6 5 4

This book is dedicated to my brother, Danny Sleator, the noted computer scientist. He has given me imaginative ideas for many of my books (including this one), and I have no doubt that someday we will write one together.

**1**

Funny things were going on inside my school locker.

First there was the note that appeared there one morning in February, a folded piece of paper taped to the inside of the door. But no one else knew the combination. The lock had not been broken, the door did not seem tampered with. I unfolded the piece of paper. On it was written:

Laura,

Mr. Dixon is giving a surprise quiz tomorrow, so be sure to study chapter 10 in the Biology book. I know you want to do well so you can get into medical school.

Signed,
A friend

At first I could make no sense out of it. Then I recognized the word at the top right-hand corner. It was my name, written backwards, with all the letters reversed—mirror writing. Maybe that was why it had been taped right under the little mirror I had hung inside the door so I could make sure my hair and makeup looked okay. I held the note up to the mirror.

Laura,
Mr. Dixon is giving a surprise quiz tomorrow, so be sure to study chapter 10 in the Biology book. I know you want to do well so you can get into medical school.
Signed,
A friend

"What's the matter, Laura? You look like you've seen a ghost," Pete said, coming up behind me.

I almost jumped. "Nothing," I said, quickly crumpling up the note. But I was a little frightened now. I did not recognize the handwriting on the note. It was strange enough that this unknown person knew about the surprise quiz—though I supposed there were ways a kid could find out something like that. But what was really unnerving was the part about medical school. Nobody, not even my parents, knew I wanted to be a doctor. Not to mention, how had the note gotten into my locker in the first place? And why was it in mirror writing? I didn't like it.

But I didn't say anything about the note to Pete. He was the most popular boy in the class, handsome and athletic and taller than me. I had been the tallest girl in junior high and had never had a boyfriend. Now, in tenth grade, I seemed to be turning out to be pretty after all. And Pete had walked home with me twice after school and had started calling me up in the evenings. But I had to be careful with him. I didn't want him to connect me with anything peculiar.

When Pete called up that night and asked me what I was doing, I said I was studying—but *not* that I was studying chapter 10 in the biology book.

"You're always studying," he said. "Maybe that's why you're so serious. You ought to loosen up more, have more fun, like your friend Arlene. She's always laughing about something."

I restrained my impulse to tell him to call her up, then, if she was so amusing. Instead I said, "You just haven't had a chance to see my crazy side. I bet you'd be surprised."

"Yeah?" he said.

The next day there was a test. Everybody complained about it. I got a perfect score, but I told Pete and Arlene I did as badly as they had. Obviously, neither of them had left the note. But who else would have? It was baffling.

After school that day I went to the hardware store and bought a new lock. It was a different kind, cylindrical, with four dials to turn. You could pick any four numbers you wanted and set it so that only those numbers would open the lock—meaning you could change the combination if anyone else found out what it was. And the man at the store assured me that it wasn't possible for someone to crack this lock by fiddling with the dials.

Then, two days later—the day the big biology report was due —the doorbell rang while I was eating breakfast. It was Pete. I was so flustered that I left the report on the breakfast table. I didn't even realize I had forgotten it until Pete dropped me off at my locker.

Then I saw I didn't have it. I groaned. There was no time to go home and get it. It was a lab report on the frog we had dissected, and I'd done a lot of work on it, making beautiful drawings of all the organs, redoing it several times until it was perfect. I'd made sure to have it ready on time. I had to do well in science if I was going to get into medical school.

And now I had left it at home. I clearly remembered it

sitting there on the kitchen table. Of course Mr. Dixon would never believe me. He was the kind of teacher who'd just think the report wasn't ready. I felt like crying as I turned the four dials and pulled open the locker.

And there was the report, lying on the metal shelf at the top.

But it couldn't be. I knew I had left it on the breakfast table. Feeling a little dazed, I picked it up. Typed neatly on the back cover was ⅤⅠ TЯOꟼƎЯ BA⅃. Inside, the entire report was backwards, the type running from right to left, all the letters, and drawings, reversed.

"No!" I shouted. It was my report all right. But I hadn't done it backwards. No typewriter wrote that way. It was impossible, like being in some kind of horrible nightmare. I threw the report back inside the locker as if it were burning my fingers. Without thinking, I slammed the door and spun the dials, the way I used to on the lock I'd had before.

An instant later I realized what I had done. I had changed the combination without looking at the numbers. Now I didn't know what the combination was. I couldn't get the report out of the locker. And even an impossible reversed report was better than no report at all.

I carefully turned the dials, hoping the previous combination would still work. It didn't. The bell rang. I groaned again and kicked the locker.

"What's the matter, Laura?"

It was Omar, the boy who had moved in next door to me.

"Oh, I can't get this stupid locker open," I said, "and my report's inside. Dixon is going to kill me."

"Go to biology class," Omar said. "I'll get the report for you."

I sighed and rolled my eyes. "Cut it out, Omar. Don't bother me now."

He gave me a long look. "I'll get it for you," he said quietly. "Go on, or you'll be late."

"So will you," I said, but I took off down the hall. I didn't want to be late as well as minus my report.

Then it hit me. Maybe it was Omar who had left me the note and put the report inside the locker—Mom could have given it to him on his way to school. It was infuriating that a creep like Omar had been invading my private space. Still, if he really could break into the locker, he would save me in biology. I spun around to see what he was doing with the lock.

But Omar had vanished.

# 2

Omar had moved next door to us over Christmas vacation. Mr. Campanelli, a withered old man who was at least eighty, had lived there by himself as long as anyone could remember. He had told Mom, on one of the rare occasions when she ran into him on the street, that a distant cousin of his whose parents had died would be coming to live with him. Mom was curious and felt sorry for the kid. The day after he arrived, she suggested that I invite him over to watch TV or play a game on my new Macintosh.

I didn't feel like going over there and pushing myself at some strange boy whose parents had just died. What would I say to him? It would be awkward and embarrassing. I wanted to ask her why he couldn't watch TV at Mr. Campanelli's—except that Mr. Campanelli probably didn't even have a TV. He was a strange, foreign old man who kept away from people. He emerged from seclusion only periodically, to lead the fight against the state highway commission, which kept wanting to tear down our block to build a highway interchange. In any case, Mom would think it was horribly selfish of me to refuse to be friendly to this poor kid who had suddenly become an orphan. So I sighed, and gritted my teeth, and trudged over there.

Even if Mr. Campanelli hadn't kept his shades closed all the time, you wouldn't have been able to see inside because of the thick, unkempt pine trees that grew right up against all the windows of the old stucco house. The place looked as though it hadn't been painted in years. I rang the bell, feeling apprehensive. I waited.

The door opened a crack, and a dark brown eye peered out at me. There were no wrinkles around it, so I figured this had to be the kid Mom had seen.

"Hi, my name is Laura. I live next door," I said. "I thought . . . maybe you might want to come over and, uh, watch TV or something."

"Huh . . . Oh, yes," he said, and popped out of the house without even getting a jacket. He slammed the door behind him so fast that I couldn't get a glimpse of what was inside.

"My name's Omar." He spoke with a slight accent, and he looked foreign, with olive skin and a long dark shock of hair that kept falling into his right eye. He was definitely plump, and about six inches shorter than me. There was a big gap on the right side of his mouth, where he was missing a tooth. It gave his face a clownish look.

"Well, come on," I said, since he was just standing there poking his tongue through the gap where his right tooth was missing, staring past my shoulder. "If there isn't anything on TV, maybe I could show you the new Macintosh I got for Christmas."

"What's a Macintosh?" he asked, plodding behind me across the snow-covered lawn. He was wearing funny-looking sandals, I noticed, in the middle of winter. And he had never heard of a Macintosh. *A weirdo,* I said to myself.

But for somebody who had never seen a personal computer before, Omar caught on really fast. By the time Mom brought in a snack, he had beaten me twice at Interstellar Pig, and I was ready for a break.

He took a suspicious nibble of a chocolate chip cookie, and then gobbled the rest of it in about a second. "That was *wonderful!*" he said. "What kind of cake is it?"

"It's not a *cake,* it's a cookie. Chocolate chip." I handed him the plate. "You've never had a chocolate chip cookie before?"

He shook his head, shoving another one into his mouth.

"Where do you come from, anyway?" I asked him. I couldn't imagine a place where they didn't have chocolate chip cookies.

"Well, I was born in Switzerland," he said reluctantly. "But we moved to this country a few years ago so my parents could take over my grandfather's business."

He didn't hesitate or look away from me when he mentioned his parents, just as though they were still alive.

"What kind of business?"

"Oh, nothing very interesting." He turned back to the computer. "Can it play any other games?"

Mom got me to invite him over a couple more times during the vacation. He was good at computer games—a little too good, since he beat me most of the time. He was amazed by things like rock videos and the electric can opener and microwave oven. He never invited me over to Mr. Campanelli's house, and he said very little about his family. I was glad about that. I didn't want him to talk about his parents dying. But I did think it was strange that he didn't seem at all depressed or moody, the way an ordinary person who had just lost his family would. He never talked about what he and Mr. Campanelli did all day in that big old house; all he would say was that Mr. Campanelli was "nice." We didn't become friends, as far as I was concerned. How can you get to know somebody who never says anything about himself?

After vacation, it turned out that he was in our class at school. I didn't talk to him much, because I didn't want anybody to connect me with a strange boy like Omar. A couple of times, when Pete was at basketball practice, Omar tried to walk home with me, but I always found some excuse to be going somewhere else. He caught on soon enough and left me alone. He was too meek to be a pest—though occasionally I noticed him watching me. Sometimes I felt a little guilty, but I told myself he was probably used to being an outcast. And anyway, why was it *my* responsibility to befriend the new kid? Pete was the boy I was interested in, and I didn't want him to get any ideas about me and Omar.

And then came the day I locked my report in my locker, and Omar offered to get it out.

*The dumb jerk,* I said to myself when I turned back to see how he got into the locker. What a stupid thing to do, pretending he could open it and then running away. I raced into class, trying to figure out how to make Mr. Dixon believe the truth.

But Omar was in the room before I'd had a chance to tell Mr. Dixon anything. He dropped the report on my desk. The title was on the front cover again, going the right way. I was so amazed I didn't even worry what anybody would think about Omar having my report.

"How'd you *do* that, Omar?"

"Take your places. I hope you all have your reports," Mr. Dixon brayed.

"See you," Omar lisped, backing away.

I stared at him, feeling uneasy. There was something the matter with his face.

I kept looking at Omar's face during class. It *seemed* the same, the shock of hair falling over his eye, the missing tooth. There was nothing obviously different. Yet every time I glanced at him I was filled by a strange sense of wrongness.

One thing I did know was that Omar was the one who had left me the note and put the report in my locker. I didn't know how he got into the locker, I didn't know how he found out the things he did—or why the jerk had picked *me* to play his little tricks on. But today I was going to find out. And make him stop.

Pete had basketball practice that afternoon. I followed Omar until he was far enough away from school so that no one would see us together. Then I called out to him.

He turned. The startling sensation hit me again. Something was wrong with his face. I couldn't pinpoint what it was—and yet it was so very different in some way that my anger suddenly drained away. I was a little frightened again.

"Omar, you put that note in my locker, didn't you?" I demanded when I reached him. "And you put my report in there too."

He wouldn't look at me directly. "Note . . . ?" he said.

"Come on, Omar. It *had* to be you. You got my report out." I didn't say anything about the report being in mirror writing —I must have imagined that. "How did you do it? And what's the combination now?"

"Combination?" he said. "I don't know."

"Then how did you get it open?"

He shrugged and pushed the hair out of his left eye. "I just fiddled with it, jiggled the door. I have a feeling for it. It's like the way some people can name any note you sing. I've always been good at getting inside—I mean, good at opening things."

"Well, if you won't tell me, then tomorrow you're going to have to *show* me. Okay?"

"I don't know." He shook his head, and the hair fell over his eye again. He brushed it away.

I stared at him. "Hey, how come all of a sudden you're parting your hair on the left? It always used to fall into your *right* eye."

"Did it?" He tried to laugh, but it sounded more like a cough. "I guess sometimes it goes to the right, and sometimes to the left."

"That's funny," I said. "My hair always goes in the same direction."

He couldn't think of anything to say. He poked his tongue into the gap where his left tooth was missing, still avoiding my eyes.

His left tooth . . .

But it was his *right* tooth that had always been missing, not his left. And I was sure his hair had always fallen into his right eye.

That was what was wrong with his face. It was reversed, turned around. Everything was on the opposite side from where it had been before.

# 3

He looked really worried now, watching my face. "I think I have to go," he said. "I'm in a hurry." He moved quickly away.

I stood and looked after him. Was I imagining things? But I knew he had always been missing his right tooth, and his hair had fallen into his right eye. I had noticed those features many times.

And now they had moved to the other side of his face.

Maybe there were two Omars, twins, one with a left-sided face and the other with a right-sided face. But there was only one Omar in school. And I knew that Omar's face had gone to the right earlier today when he had approached me at my locker and offered to get my report. Less than a minute later, when he had shown up in class with the report, his face had been reversed. It didn't make any sense.

And there were other things almost as amazing as the reversal of his face. Getting into the locker without knowing the combination. The information in the note. My report being reversed, which I now knew I had not imagined. What was the connection?

Part of me was frightened and repelled. Omar wasn't just a plain old jerk anymore. What had happened to him was unnatural, monstrous. He was like someone with a terrible disease— someone you should stay away from.

But at the same time I was wildly curious. Was he twins, or had he undergone a magical transformation? There had to be an explanation. And the explanation might be the most miraculous part of all.

My curiosity won. I told myself that I didn't have to get very close to him, in case whatever was wrong with him was catching. But I *did* have to get him to tell me the whole story, or I really would go nuts.

I caught up with him. "Omar, would you like to come over for some cookies? Or to play with my computer? You're not really in a hurry, are you?"

He sighed pitifully. "I . . . I don't know. I probably shouldn't."

"Come on. It'll be fun."

He stared down at the sidewalk.

"Omar. Tell me the truth. Are you really twins?"

"No, I'm not twins," he said, looking directly up into my eyes now.

"Then your face did reverse," I whispered.

He breathed deeply. "You think I'm a freak, don't you?" He twisted his mouth. "I didn't think you would notice what happened to my face. No one has before."

"I noticed. And now you have to tell me all about it. And

about the note, and how you knew that stuff. Don't you *want* to tell somebody? Isn't that why you left the note in the first place?"

"Well . . ." He hesitated. "I . . . I *did* hope maybe we were going to be friends, at first. And then school started, and . . . you wouldn't talk to me anymore. And then, I just wanted to help you out. That's why I left you the note, and got your report. It didn't seem right not to help you. But I shouldn't have. It was stupid. It was dangerous."

"But why can't you tell me how you did it?"

He groaned. "I can't, Laura. I just *can't.* It's too risky."

"But that's not *fair!*" I said, angrily tossing back my long hair. "You started it. It's your own fault I'm so curious now. Come on, Omar."

"No!" he insisted, lifting his chin.

I hadn't expected him to be so stubborn about it. Why was it so important to keep it a secret? I was more curious than ever now. I glared at him, wondering what I could do to persuade him. Then it hit me. "Well, if you really *did* want to be my friend, you'd tell me," I said.

That seemed to surprise him. His mouth opened slightly, but he didn't speak.

Maybe I was on the right track. "If you knew what it meant to be friends, you'd know friends don't keep secrets from each other."

"But we're not friends. Friends don't avoid each other at school."

"We *could* be friends," I said hastily. "I had fun those times you came over during vacation. Didn't *you?*"

"Well . . . yes, sure I did," he said, his eyes sliding away from me. "But that doesn't—I mean . . ."

He seemed so vulnerable at that moment that I almost felt sorry for him. But I could see he was weakening, and pressed on. "Look, just come on over now. You *have* to tell me more.

And we *will* be friends." I crossed my fingers behind my back. "I promise."

"But . . ."

I smiled at him. *"Please,* Omar?"

He sighed again, then said, very quietly, "Well, would you promise not to tell *anybody* what . . . what I tell—"

"Yes, yes, I promise!" I said, not even waiting for him to finish.

"Well, we have to shake on it, then."

I rolled my eyes. "Why are you making such a big deal out of it?"

"Because it *is* a big deal. You promise, Laura?" He stuck out his hand.

I grabbed his hand and pumped it. "Yes, yes, I promise, Omar. My word of honor, my sacred oath, anything else you can think of. I promise. Okay?"

"Okay. Then . . . I'll tell you," Omar said.

I dragged him into the house and up to my room. "Okay, spill it," I demanded.

"I need some paper and a pencil and a scissors," he said.

"Why can't you just tell me?"

"Because I have to *show* you, or you won't understand. Do you really want to understand it or not?"

I got him the paper and pencil and scissors, and pulled two chairs up to my desk, and pushed the junk on it out of the way. "I still don't know why you can't just tell me," I said.

"Because it's really hard to picture it unless you have examples, analogies, to look at."

"Hard to picture what?"

"The fourth dimension," he said.

# 4

He began cutting a shape out of a piece of paper. "Now, what I'm going to show you is the difference between a flat, two-dimensional world and the three-dimensional world we live in," he said, sounding like a little lisping professor. "That will help you understand what it's like for me to go into the fourth dimension."

"Oh, come off it, Omar," I said. "The fourth dimension is just an hypothetical math concept. Or else it's time, or something. Just a lot of sci-fi crud. You expect me to believe that?"

He looked at me. "Do you believe what happened to my face —and all the rest of me?"

I didn't have an answer.

"Put your ear against my chest," he said.

"What for?" I asked, backing my chair away from him.

"I just want you to listen to my heart," he explained patiently. "Do you really want to understand this or not?"

"Well . . . okay." I leaned forward and put my ear against the left side of his chest, where the heart is.

"I can't hear anything," I said finally. I wondered if he were some kind of a robot without a heart at all.

"Try the other side."

"But . . ." I was about to protest that the heart is always on the left side of the body. Then I was struck by the obvious. I pressed my ear against the right side of his chest. There it was, thumping away, directly opposite where it should have been.

"Now, are you going to believe me about the fourth dimension?"

What could I say? Nothing he could tell me would be any harder to believe than a person's heart being on the wrong side of his body. It wasn't just his features that had reversed—it was everything else about him too.

"Yes, I believe you," I said. "Please just get on with it."

"Okay. Now try to imagine a two-dimensional world. It's flat, like this piece of paper. The people who live there are flat too, like paper dolls. On the surface of the paper they can go up and down and from side to side. But they can't come up *off* the paper, or go down underneath it. That would be going into the third dimension. They're like comic-strip characters, stuck to the page."

"All right, I get the picture. But what does that have to do with your body changing sides—or how you opened my locker? I want to know *exactly* how you did that."

"I'm telling you." He drew a square on the paper, four thick connected lines. Next to the square he drew a stick figure. Then he put a little scrap of paper inside the square. "Now, this is two-dimensional Laura, and her two-dimensional locker, with the report inside it. 2-D Laura can't go through these solid lines; they're solid walls to her. So there's no way she can get into the locker."

"Go on."

"All right. Now here comes 2-D Omar." He pushed a crude, cutout figure across the page. It was a person in profile, facing to the left, with a big nose. "Now, Omar wants to help Laura get the report out of the locker. And Omar can do something Laura doesn't know how to do. He can go into the third dimension. So if he went into the third dimension, where does the figure go?"

"I guess . . . up off the sheet of paper."

"That's right." He lifted the cutout off the paper and moved it over until it was directly above the square. "And from the third dimension, the locker looks to him the way it looks to us—he can see *over* the walls. Omar can easily reach into the closed locker from 3-space and get the report without even opening the locker. He just goes over and reaches in. Makes sense?"

"Yeah . . . I guess it does."

He took the scrap of paper out of the square and put it on the cutout's hand. Then he moved the cutout back to the right side of the square and put it down on the paper. "Then Omar goes back into 2-space, and gives Laura the report." He looked at me and smiled. "See? And it works just the same way if a 3-D person like me can go into the *fourth* dimension. From out there, I can just reach into things, without opening them. That's how I got the report out of your locker. I didn't have to bother trying to open it."

"Wait a minute." Yes, I could see how a flat 2-D person, if he were somehow able to lift himself up off the page, could reach into a closed square without opening it. But it wasn't so easy to imagine a 3-D person like Omar lifting himself somewhere *out* of our space and reaching into my closed locker.

"But where is it?" I asked him. "Where is 'up' out of 3-space? I can't picture it."

"Because you've never been there. That's why I have to explain it in 2- and 3-space, instead of 3 and 4."

I was still skeptical. "But how about the way your left and right sides got switched? Show me how that works."

"Nothing to it." He sounded more sure of himself than I'd ever heard him. He slid the cutout figure with the left-facing profile nose around on the paper. "As long as 2-D Omar is stuck in 2-space, on the flat page, he's always going to be facing to the left. But Omar can lift himself up into 3-space." He held the figure above the paper. "And what would happen if he turned over in 3-space? Something that could never happen on the flat page." He flipped the figure over onto its other side. Now the nose pointed to the right. "And then he went back into 2-space?" He set the figure back down on the paper, the nose pointing to the right. "He would be the reverse of what he had been before—his own mirror image. Now do you understand?" He sat back in his chair and folded his arms.

"You got . . . flipped over in 4-space?" I said, keeping as far away from him as the small desk would allow.

He nodded, and gestured with his left hand. "See, when I tossed the report in there before, it must have flipped over in 4-space as it fell, and got reversed. So when I went in to get it, I picked it up and then turned around in 4-space, to *un-* reverse the report—and that reversed me."

"But how did you know I'd left the report at home? Did Mom ask you to bring it to school?"

"No. I just . . . peeked inside your house when I was walking past. And I saw that you'd forgotten it. And I couldn't stand to think of what was going to happen to you in school. So I just went into your house, from 4-space, and got it. I probably shouldn't have."

"But didn't Mom and Dad see you?"

"They were there, but they couldn't see me. When I'm in 4-space, I'm outside of people's field of vision."

"You mean . . . you're *invisible*?"

"Not exactly." He shifted in his chair. "I mean, if people knew what to look for, they might notice the part of me that was sticking into 3-space. But most people don't know what to look for."

"That means you could do practically *anything*," I said. If I hadn't had proof, I wouldn't have believed any of this. But I had plenty of proof, and I was getting excited. "What's it like out there, Omar? What does it feel like? What does everything *look* like? And . . . could you ever bring somebody else out there with you?"

"No. I won't do that." He pushed his chair back hastily and got up, backing away from me. "I have to go now. And please, don't ever ask me to take you . . . out there. Please don't, Laura. See you later." And he left.

But I had already persuaded him to give in once, and I was sure I could do it again.

# 5

After he left, I sat and thought.

Now I could figure out how Omar had collected the information on the note he had left in my locker. Obviously, he had gone into 4-space to examine the contents of Mr. Dixon's desk and had seen his lesson plan for the next day. Sneaky. And he must have been watching me for a while, in my room, where I pored over my paperback of Gray's *Anatomy*, and sometimes even wrote out my name, *Dr. Laura Abrams, M.D.* That was the only way he could have found out I wanted to be a doctor.

I was glad I had learned about 4-space and Omar's abilities. And yet I was even more uneasy now than I had been before.

He could sneak around, outside my field of vision, watching and listening, as good as invisible. He might be watching me right this minute. The idea of it made me horribly uncomfortable.

There was only one way I could ever be sure of privacy again. If I was able to go into 4-space myself, then I could check around to see whether Omar was spying on me. And if I was ever going to get Omar to show me the way, then I would have to convince him, more than I already had, that we really were friends. I was more determined than ever now. I began the next day, by going over to his house and asking him to walk to school with me.

Once again he opened his door only wide enough to squeeze out, preventing me from seeing inside. And he seemed a little embarrassed in my presence, as if he was afraid he'd told me too much about himself. I was a bit edgy too, worrying that Pete might see us together and wondering how I would explain it to him.

"Anything you, uh, want me to help you out with today?" Omar asked me when we were about halfway to school. I hadn't been saying much, and neither had he.

"Help me out?" I said, not sure what he meant.

"Well . . . I guess you know what I can do now. So do you want to know the answers to any homework problems, or what the teachers are saying?"

"Well, as a matter of fact, there *is* something I'd like to know," I told him.

"Okay. What is it?"

"How did you learn how to get into 4-space?"

He looked away from me. "I . . . I can't tell you that."

"I thought we were friends, Omar. And friends tell each other things."

"You haven't told me anything about yourself," he said.

"What is there for me to tell you? I don't have special powers like you do. I'm just an ordinary person."

"You could tell me about any problems you have, like with your family," he said slowly. "Or if it bothers you being the tallest girl in the class. Or about Pete."

I sighed. Why did Omar have to be so peculiar? No other kid would want to pry into such difficult and personal things. "I thought you already knew all about me—from sneaking around and spying where I couldn't see you."

"Spying?" he said, as though I had insulted him. "But I wasn't spying, Laura. And I can't read minds. I don't know what your feelings are. And sometimes it's good to talk about your feelings. I'm just trying to help."

I did my best to control my irritation. I wanted him to think I was his friend, after all. "Well, I appreciate your interest, Omar. But there isn't time to get into those things right now. We'll be there in a minute."

We walked into the schoolyard. It was full of kids, and I felt horribly conspicuous with Omar. Pete and Arlene were not here yet, I was relieved to see. But they would show up at any minute.

"Come on, Omar, you have to help me with my locker," I said, and hurried him into the building.

"I can probably figure out the new combination if I look at it from the inside," he said, stopping by the boys' bathroom.

"But my locker's over here."

"Yes, but I have to go into 4-space from someplace where nobody can see me. I'll meet you at your locker."

When I got there, the dials on the lock were already turning on their own. A minute later the lock clicked open. Omar came trotting along the corridor as the first bell rang. "The combination is 4-3-2-7," he said. "I have to get to my locker now, or I'll be late."

Pete stopped at my desk before Mr. Dixon called the class to order. "Have a nice walk to school this morning?" he said lightly.

"Not particularly," I said, with a grimace.

"I dropped over to get you, but you'd already left with that Omar jerk." He didn't seem offended, just puzzled and a little disapproving. "I don't get it."

"Oh, it's just because he lives next door, and my mom feels sorry for him and everything," I explained, trying to keep my voice down so Omar wouldn't hear.

Pete shrugged. "Oh. Well, anyway, see you at lunch." The final bell rang.

But when I emerged from the cafeteria line with Pete and Arlene, there was Omar, sitting at one end of a long, empty table. He smiled faintly at me, then looked away.

"Hey, you guys, let's sit over there," I said, unable to sound very enthusiastic.

"With *Omar*?" said Arlene, appalled. "Are you kidding?"

"Oh, come on, just this once. Do me a favor," I said. "He's not that bad. He's more interesting than he looks."

"So's my brother's pet gerbil. Anyway, what would everybody think?" Arlene moved off toward a more crowded table.

"Aren't you getting a little carried away with this charity business?" Pete asked me, not smiling.

"I just don't want to be mean and keep snubbing him all the time," I said. "Sure, I'd rather sit with the others. Just do it for me. You know nobody would dare put *you* down for sitting with him."

"You mean you're actually going to leave me just standing here to go sit with *him*? In front of everybody?" He was angry now, his face flushed.

"But, Pete, I didn't think you would—"

He turned and waved at somebody and strolled away.

He thought I was rejecting him. And what seemed to bother him the most was that I was choosing a pitiful person like Omar, with everybody watching. He probably would have preferred me to go sit with one of his jock friends—it would have been less demeaning. I was amazed.

It was an effort not to slam my tray on the table when I sat down across from Omar. I was suddenly furious at Pete and Arlene for deserting me. I had never realized how petty and unbending they were.

"Laura," Omar said softly, "you should go sit with them. I don't mind eating alone."

"Who wants to?" I said. If I left him now I'd be as mean as the others were. "Anyway, if they sat with us, we couldn't talk about 4-space. And if they don't like it, that's tough."

But after school, when I stood at my locker and watched Pete and Arlene walk out of the building together, my stomach sank. I had been hoping for a week that Pete would ask me to the spring dance. Now that didn't seem very likely.

I ran into Omar just outside the schoolyard, where he'd obviously been waiting. It was too late now for me to worry about anybody seeing us together. The damage had already been done.

He spoke rather flatly, not looking at me, as though he had been planning what he was going to say. "Laura . . . I appreciate what you did at lunch. You were great."

I didn't tell him that my motivation had been purely selfish. I wanted to get him to take me into 4-space. "I just thought . . . that's what a friend would do," I said, and sighed.

"But what's the matter?" he said, worried. "They forgave you for sitting with me, didn't they?"

"Not exactly," I said. He was so concerned, I had the momentary impulse to lie and tell him everything was okay just so he wouldn't feel so bad—but I knew he wouldn't believe me.

"It's just that Pete didn't talk to me all afternoon. And now he's gone off with Arlene."

"Is it because he's jealous? Does he think you're going out with *me*?" He seemed to like that idea.

"No, Omar." I was pretty sure Pete didn't think anything like that.

"But . . . you mean he's still mad at you just because you *sat* with me in the cafeteria?" Omar said, as if he could hardly believe it.

I shrugged. "I guess so."

"But that doesn't make sense." Omar slowly shook his head, baffled. "Shouldn't he *like* you for being decent to me? And for not being controlled by what the other kids think? Does he expect you to do just what he wants all the time?"

"You don't understand, Omar!" I said, my voice rising. I was angry because I knew Omar was right, that if Pete were a better person he wouldn't have reacted against me. But I also knew that I wanted to go out with Pete anyway, just because he was so good-looking and because of the status he would give me. And maybe it *was* petty of me, but that was how I felt.

"I'm sorry, Laura," Omar said, his shoulders slumping mournfully. "I'd do anything to make you feel better. Just tell me how to do it, and I will."

It was my chance, and I grabbed it. "Take me into 4-space with you," I said.

He stopped walking. The blood drained from his face. "Not that. You don't understand. It's . . . dangerous," he said faintly.

"But you said you'd do anything, Omar. And that's the only thing that would make me feel better."

"But . . . I'm not allowed to."

"But what about *me*, Omar?" I said, dismissing his excuse. "I didn't worry about what other people wanted me to do when

I sat with you at lunch. I just did it because we're friends. And now I'm the one who feels awful, and it's your turn to help me out."

"But this . . . isn't the same."

"Please, Omar," I begged him. "Here I am, asking you to help me, and you keep making these excuses. It's just one little favor, and it means so much to me. That's what friends are for. I'd be so grateful. You'd be one of my best friends forever. Doesn't that mean anything to you at all?"

"It *does*, Laura," he said, in a kind of agony. "But . . ."

"Then take me, Omar. Otherwise, why should I believe you care about me at all?"

He gazed up at me miserably, standing there on the sidewalk. "I *do* care about you, Laura. It's just that . . ." He glanced away for a moment. He shook his head, then looked up at me again.

"Well, I could care about you too, Omar," I said, aware that I was leading him on, but too eager to worry about that now. I touched his arm. *"Please?"*

"Well . . ." He closed his eyes, almost as if he were praying. "Uh . . . okay," he whispered, and opened his eyes. "I'll . . . take you."

"Oh, thank you, Omar. Thank you so much! I'll never forget this. I mean it. Come on, let's go."

"But I have to go get my equipment first. And we mustn't go there from out here on the street," he said hastily. "We have to go from your house."

"Why?"

"Because if we're inside your house, they won't be as likely to notice us," he said, a funny look on his face. "And we don't want them to notice us."

"But there's no other kids around. We could take off from behind those trees."

"I don't mean other kids," he said.

"Then who *do* you mean?"

"The ones out there," he said, barely audibly. "The 4-space creatures."

## b

I waited impatiently at home while Omar ran next door to get whatever his equipment was, afraid he was just trying to get out of taking me. But he showed up in five minutes, wearing mountain-climbing boots and an elaborate leather harness on his back with a fat loop of clothesline attached to it.

"How come you didn't need all that stuff at school this morning?"

"Because you weren't coming with me, and I was only reaching into your locker." He pulled a small flashlight out of his pocket.

"What's the flashlight for?"

"You need light to see into dark places, even from 4-space."

"Want a cookie or anything, before we go?" I asked him.

"Oh, no," he said. "It wouldn't taste good this way."

It was a strange remark. Omar loved cookies. And what did he mean by *this way*? But I was too preoccupied to pay much attention to it, and I didn't want a cookie myself. "These 4-space creatures," I said, up in my room with the door closed. "Do you mean they're dangerous? Monsters?"

"I don't know if they're *monsters*, exactly," he said, tilting his head to the side, his hair falling over his left eye. "I think they might be kind of like people, actually."

"Can't you tell? Are they invisible or something?"

"No. They're easy to see. It's just hard to figure out what they look like."

"I don't know what you're talking about."

"I think you'll understand better afterwards."

"But how come you don't want them to notice us?" I pressed him.

"I just think it's better to start from someplace private, in case we have to get back in a hurry—especially on your first trip."

His vagueness about the conditions out there was unsettling. Why couldn't he give me a straight answer about something so important? "Omar, just tell me, yes or no: Are they dangerous or aren't they?"

"We don't want them to see us, Laura. For one thing we're like paper dolls to them. They could pick us up and roll us into a tube, or fold us into a paper airplane and throw us at something."

I was beginning to wonder if I really wanted to make the trip at all.

"And for another thing . . . if they catch us, we have to die." He looked at me solemnly.

"You're just trying to scare me, Omar!"

"No. But they do tend to stay away from the space that's

directly *ana* and *kata* from our houses. So it's safer to do it from inside."

"What are *ana* and *kata*?"

"The two directions above and below our space, at right angles to all our directions." He studied my face. "Want to change your mind?" he asked hopefully.

"I'm fine. I want to go now." If Omar dared to go out there, then how could I admit to being afraid? Anyway, he had done it over and over again, and hadn't been rolled up or folded yet —or killed for getting caught. "Maybe just a quick trip," I added.

"Good." He took the end of the coil of rope, squatted down and tied it firmly around one of the legs of my desk.

"Why are you doing that?"

"So we can find our way back, in case we get lost." He stood up and hooked a strap from his harness around one of my belt loops. "Take my hand, Laura." He reached out his left hand, and I took it with my right. His hand was unpleasantly moist. "We won't go far. We'll just look around your room. But still, no matter what happens, you must *not* let go of my hand. You got that, Laura? Do *not* let go."

"Why not? What about this strap?"

"Straps can get unhooked. And if we got separated, you could easily get lost. And you might never find your way back. And I might never be able to find you. It's big out there, and it's complicated. If I lost you . . . It's too terrible even to think about. Do you promise not to let go?"

"Yes, yes, I promise."

He squeezed my hand. "Here we go."

Omar bent his knees and lifted his arms like a plump little Superman preparing to take off. I did the same. His face reddened and a vein stood out on his forehead. He tilted over in a sideways direction. Then his body was stretching out at an impossible angle. He rippled and pulsated like a reflection in a distorting mirror. He grunted.

The floor lurched and tilted away. I closed my eyes. It was like falling down an unexpected stairway in the darkness. Dizziness slammed through me. My stomach jumped. My fingers loosened and began to slip away from Omar's.

He gripped my hand harder. We weren't falling. The dizziness stopped.

"Open your eyes, Laura," Omar said.

I opened them. Instantly I squeezed them shut, moaning, dizzier than before.

"Take it slow, Laura. Try not to move your head. You'll get used to it."

Cautiously, my heart pounding, I opened my eyes again.

My bedroom floor hung directly above me. I saw the woven pattern of the rag rug, the grain of the floorboards. There was a dark, dusty area to one side that didn't look familiar, until I noticed the dim cover of an old romance comic that had fallen under my desk. Next to the comic book, a black column about three inches thick stretched off to the left and right. On the other side of the column I could see a bright pattern of blue-and-white octagons. It took me a moment to realize it was the bathroom floor.

"Keep your eyes fixed in one place, Laura," Omar said, invisible beside me. "You okay?"

"But nothing makes sense! I can hardly tell what I'm looking at."

"That's because you don't have 4-D eyes, so you can only see a 3-D cross section of 4-space. When you move your eyes, you'll see a different section. You have to learn how to put them all together. Now, move your head just a tiny bit."

I turned my head about an inch. There was a confusing moment of things rushing past. Then another picture stabilized. Where the floor underneath my desk had been was a solid black rectangle. The bright space above it was empty, except for a round white basin filled with liquid. But most of what I now saw was blackness.

"Now it's too dark to see," I whined.

"I told you, you can't see inside things without light," Omar said. "That's why I always have my pocket flashlight." I felt him move beside me, then heard a click.

Now, instead of a black rectangle, I saw a confusing jumble of objects in separate compartments, heavily outlined by shadows. I began to recognize pencils and rubber bands and keys, an old school workbook from last year, a pyramidlike shape of many layers that seemed to be a pile of paper viewed from some peculiar angle. And what was that wrinkled red oval thing with a thin black edge? A tube of red paint, seen from the inside and the outside at the same time.

I lifted my hand to take the tube of paint out of the desk. In the flashlight beam, I saw white bones enclosed in layered strips of pink, thin branching wires with blue liquid coursing through them.

"My hand!" I whispered. "I can see the inside of my hand!"

Then I noticed something else moving, and carefully lifted my head a fraction of an inch. It was Mom, walking into the downstairs hallway, sideways. For a second I saw her face, looking flat, like a TV picture. But I also saw her teeth, and her tongue, and her tonsils, and the beginnings of some complicated structures inside both of her ears.

I sensed Omar shifting beside me again. The desk went dark. Then Omar gasped. "Laura," he whispered. "Don't look over at— We better go."

"Don't look at what?" It had been amazing to see the inside of my hand and Mom's head. "Don't look at what, Omar? You have to tell me!"

"You're not ready. Time to go."

"Tell me!" I jerked and turned toward what I thought was

the direction his voice was coming from. Everything shifted and spun. Now I stared down at the ceiling of my room. Little black bugs crawled around inside the opaque light fixture. To the left was a thick boundary, and beyond it, the bare branches of the tree outside the house, upside down.

But I was beginning to get used to the surprises now. "Tell me, Omar! Look at what? I'm ready."

"At . . . him," he murmured. "I mean, one of them. Oh, my gosh!"

"Where? Show me! I'm ready."

"You think so?" he said, as though I didn't know what I was talking about. "All right, Laura. I'll show you. But we don't have much time."

I felt something inside my nose, gently turning me in a direction that was, somehow, completely unexpected. Everything rushed around more wildly than ever.

I heard music, a deep voice singing in the distance. "Tra la-la la! Tra la-la la!"

"There he is, Laura."

I blinked. I wasn't looking inside my room anymore, or outside the house, or at anything in the world.

I stared down a long avenue of jagged, irregular shapes. They flickered and changed, sparkling in a bluish light that was not sunlight. They were all sizes, without pattern or meaning, and could have been jewels, or fragmented panes of glass, or some kind of crystalline plants. They might have been beautiful if they hadn't been so utterly alien.

But they were ordinary compared to the incomprehensible thing moving through them, moving toward us, as the singing voice grew louder. The thing was made of grayish flesh. Textured bands and patches of fur slid across it as it moved. But was it one thing or many? At first it had been a featureless rolling oblong. Then it split. Five narrow poles slithered in a kind of dance to the jaunty music. The poles fused together into a fat barrel shape. An eye oozed down the barrel and disappeared as the barrel expanded into a pimpled sphere. A wide red gash appeared, bordered by darker bands of flesh— a gash that could be nothing other than a mouth. "Tra la-la la! Tra la-la la!" the voice boomed out, "Little brothers, here am I! Bringing luck and jollity!" And the thing glided closer.

"Get me out of here, Omar," I whispered. "Out of here. Get me out. Now."

He didn't argue. The world reeled and we fell. The floor rushed up and grabbed my feet. I barely managed not to topple over.

"I . . . I warned you, Laura," Omar said. But he looked as shaken as I was. "I have to get home fast." He let go of my hand, unhooked the strap from my belt loop, and untied the rope from the desk.

"What *was* that thing?" I asked. "Why did it look like that?"

"I can explain, Laura," he said, ashen-faced. "But not now. Later."

"Good. I need to forget about it now."

"Don't worry, Laura," Omar said, quickly backing away toward the stairs. "We're safe from him this time, maybe." He turned and ran.

"That's nice to know," I muttered.

It was not until half an hour later, when the world had stopped tilting and I was lying on my bed, that I noticed that everything in the room was turned around, backwards.

Reversed.

# 7

It wasn't just the furniture that was in the wrong place. The window and the closet and the door had also been switched around.

I got up and leaned unsteadily over the bookcase. All the titles on the spines were in mirror writing. I looked through a couple of books. The insides were in mirror writing too. I scrabbled through the school notebooks on my desk. My own handwriting went from right to left, slanted the wrong way, every letter written backwards.

I groaned and threw myself down and turned to look out the window beside the bed, hoping that a view of the real world would stabilize me. A mistake. The house had jumped to the other side of the street. The parked cars were facing in the wrong direction. The afternoon sun was setting in the east.

I curled up and closed my eyes. There was only one explanation. I must have flipped over in 4-space. Now *I* was reversed.

Omar hadn't told me it was like this—that to a reversed person, the whole world seemed to be turned around. But it made sense. My right eye was now seeing what my left eye usually saw and vice versa. It was perfectly logical.

I lay there taking slow, deep breaths, which I had heard was supposed to calm you down. I looked around the room again, trying to adjust. Why did I have to be so upset? Omar could handle being reversed, so I should be able to. Anyway, I wasn't permanently stuck this way. Omar could always take me out into 4-space again and turn me around.

I thought about our little trip. 4-space had not been at all what I had expected. I had imagined it would be more like the analogies Omar had used to explain it. A feeling of power, of rising off the flat page to a superior vantage point from which you could see everything, inside and out, and were able to move anywhere.

Instead, it had been a series of confusing *partial* views. I had seen inside things, but it hadn't been like looking through clear glass, as I had halfway expected. It wasn't that easy. And every time I moved my eyes, the view had changed completely. I hadn't felt powerful at all; I had felt completely lost and helpless.

All I had accomplished by manipulating Omar into taking me along with him was to end up reversed, in a mirror world.

And that wasn't even the worst part of it: There was the 4-space creature we had seen, blobbing and separating and fusing, more horrible than any nightmare because it wasn't a dream. It was real.

There were creatures like that all around us, apparently. And they didn't seem to be locked away from us in some fantasy land or separated by any kind of magic barrier wall. They were here, even though we couldn't see them. And they had complete access to our world. We were like flat creatures on a piece of paper to them, living in houses that were nothing but line drawings. They could see inside us and inside our buildings. Whenever they felt like it, they could reach down and pluck us right off the page.

I was sweating. I wanted to scream. How could I go on for another minute knowing about them?

"Keep calm," I whispered, and took a deep breath. After all, Omar knew about them too. And Omar went on living, in a somewhat normal way, from day to day. They had never done anything to him. I had never heard of them invading our world. I had to keep remembering that. It was the only way to deal with it.

Meanwhile, I had to learn how to negotiate around a mirror world, at least until tomorrow, when Omar could reverse me again. And I had to start now. It was probably almost time for supper. I looked at the clock. It was backwards, but since it said six o'clock I could read it.

I found the door and went out into the hall. I opened the bathroom door. But it was the closet. The bathroom had moved across the hall. I went in and stood against the door and looked carefully around the room, getting my bearings, so I wouldn't make any more dumb mistakes. Then I walked directly to the sink. It was comforting to see the *H* on the hot-water tap. I tried to turn on the other tap. It seemed to be stuck. Then I turned it the wrong way, and it worked. I splashed cold water on my face, looking in the mirror. The reflection was so startling that I didn't notice how funny the water smelled. The room in the mirror was the familiar bathroom I had known before, in the real world.

I automatically reached for the cup. But it was on the wrong side of the sink. My right hand was on my left side now, meaning that I was left-handed. I found the cup and filled it awkwardly. What was I going to do at supper? If I tried to eat with my knife and fork in the wrong hands, I would be so clumsy at it that Mom and Dad would notice something was the matter. I would probably draw less attention to myself by eating the way that felt natural to me, which would be the opposite of the way I usually ate. And if anybody did notice it, I could just say I was practicing how to be ambidextrous.

I lifted the cup and took a big gulp.

Then I was choking and spitting it out. The liquid in the cup tasted like leftover tuna-fish salad. The water supply must be contaminated. I kept spitting, trying to get rid of the unexpected taste, hoping I hadn't swallowed any. Then I wiped my mouth on a towel and started for the door. I had to warn Mom and Dad.

But I had forgotten to go the wrong way and ended up almost falling into the bathtub. And as I did so, I was struck by the puzzling remark Omar had made earlier. I had offered him a cookie, and he had said, "Oh, no, it wouldn't taste good this way."

Omar had been reversed when he said that. Was that what he had meant by "this way"? And was he saying, then, that everything tastes different to a person who is reversed?

I stood beside the bathtub and tried to think logically. I felt my heart beating on the right side of my chest. I knew that it wasn't just the outside that was reversed. Everything inside me was reversed too. That included all the molecules in my body, such as the molecules in my taste buds and digestive fluids, for instance. Meaning that, from my body's point of view, any substance I put into it would be treated as the reverse of itself.

I couldn't remember whether water molecules were symmetrical or not. But even if they were, I knew that drinking water was full of lots of other chemicals, purifiers, that were probably not symmetrical at all. Meaning that my body would treat them as foreign substances.

And probably all foods had asymmetrical molecules in them. Everything would taste wrong to me. I didn't have to worry about which hand to eat with. As long as I was turned around, I didn't dare to eat.

Despite my queasiness of only moments before, I was suddenly ravenous. Now that I knew I couldn't eat, my body perversely demanded to be fed. I hadn't had much lunch today, I remembered, and hardly any breakfast. I was so hungry I couldn't stand it. I'd starve if I couldn't eat until tomorrow. There was only one thing to do, and I didn't have much time before supper. I hoped no one would try to stop me.

I left the bathroom. Thinking carefully, I turned the wrong way and reached the stairs at the end of the hall. Down the stairs, into a reversed living room, where backwards Dad was reading a newspaper printed in mirror writing. I tried to move quietly, so he wouldn't notice me. Despite the loathsome stenches of the food Mom was concocting in the kitchen, I was getting hungrier by the minute. I kept my eyes fixed on the front door so I wouldn't accidentally go the right way and get delayed.

I reached the door and fumbled with the lock.

"Laura?" Mom stepped out of the kitchen. "Oh, there you are. Better set the table. We're almost ready to eat."

"But . . ." I was too rattled now to even think about setting the table backwards. And how long would it take Mom to notice that I was reversed? She knew my face better than anyone. "Okay, I will, in a minute. But first I just have to go outside, and . . . get something."

"You have to go out, right before supper?" Mom stepped

closer and stared at me, frowning. "Is something wrong? What do you mean, you have to get something?"

"Uh, the math assignment. I have to get it from Omar." I struggled with the door, but I couldn't seem to make it work.

"Can't it wait?" Mom peered at my face. "You don't look so hot, Laura."

I'd look worse if I had to sit there and eat her disgusting reversed food in front of them. "I have to get it before they eat. They go to bed early." At last I managed to get the door open. "I'll be back in *one minute,* I promise." Without waiting for an answer, I rushed outside, slammed the door, and ran across the lawn to Omar's. I rang the bell. Then I noticed that it was the wrong house. Omar's was on the other side now. I dashed back across the lawn, cursing myself for wasting time, and pressed Omar's bell.

I waited, hopping with impatience. There was no response. What if Omar couldn't change me back now? How would I get through supper, and the rest of the evening? I rang the bell again, then knocked.

At the house on the other side of mine, the porch light went on. Mr. Foster opened the door and looked around. I cringed against Omar's door. When it opened, I almost fell inside.

"Laura!" Omar whispered, looking scared. "What are you doing here?"

Music boomed out of the house.

"Quick, Omar! I'm reversed. You have to take me out there and flip me over, right away!"

"*Now?* Oh, no, I can't, Laura." He backed away, shaking his head. "He'll see us, he'll know I took you—" He pressed his lips together, still shaking his head.

What was he talking about? "But my mom and dad will find out if you *don't* change me back," I said. "I won't be able to eat. *They'll* notice I'm backwards for sure. Then it won't be

| 41

a secret anymore. What could I tell them, except the truth?"

"Your mom and dad? Tell them? No, you can't." I had never seen him so upset. His voice was getting out of control. Luckily, the loud music covered our conversation. Oddly familiar music, reminding me of something unpleasant. "Tra la-la la! Tra la-la la! Hunger is an urgent beast!" sang a rich bass voice. I happened to notice that the brightly lit living room, behind Omar, was completely empty of furniture.

But I was too frantic to think about that. "They'll notice, Omar. They'll find out. I don't know what to do. *Please!*"

He put his hands over his eyes. "Oh, *why* did I have to do that?" he moaned. "Why . . . ?" Then he flung his hands down and looked up at me. "All right. It's my own fault. We have to risk it. If we're quick enough, and if I do it right, maybe he won't catch us." He stared past me for a moment, thinking, chewing his lip. Then he stepped forward, closed the door, and pulled me past the evergreen bushes that grew against the front of his house. He crouched down in the darkness where the bushes stopped at the corner of the stucco wall, gripping my hand.

"Out here, Omar?" I asked him, frightened now. "I thought you said it was safer from the inside."

"Because it's dark here. And whatever happens, Laura, keep your eyes closed. *You must not look.* Promise?"

"Sure, Omar. But—"

"Here we go."

We were facing away from the house. I closed my eyes. Omar hiccuped. The ground fell away. My head spun.

Then I stabilized. Something reached inside my nose and pulled me around in an unexpected direction. Sudden orange light flared up behind my closed eyelids. The music was around me again. Involuntarily, my eyes blinked open.

I only looked for a second. But that was enough.

There was a thick dark column on the left that narrowed at the top somehow so that I could see right over it—the wall of Omar's house. The largest space within was nothing but bright light. But there was a smaller room that was not empty. An aluminum sink full of soapy water hung upside down above me, tilted away at an odd angle so that it looked almost diamond-shaped. I saw a stovetop, with four oval burners, and the inside of the oven, because the oven light was on. The checkered oilcloth on the table was also bent into a diamond pattern, as were the three plastic place mats, which had cartoonlike maps of the United States on them. Only a cross section of Mr. Campanelli's kitchen, seen from a weird point of view.

Except for the four-foot-thick mound of flesh that quivered and pulsed beside the tabletop. It puffed up like a balloon, glistening with moisture. A blue eye rolled across it. The thing split down the middle. Big lips opened. "Tra la-la la! Hip hurrah! Won't we have a happy time!" rumbled the bass voice.

I squeezed my eyes shut and pressed my lips together to keep from screaming. The world tilted. I fell, and landed, and cautiously opened my eyes. I was standing with Omar, beside the bushes, staring at the corner of his house.

It had been a hallucination. I had imagined the thing in the kitchen, because of hearing the same music I had heard when we saw the 4-space creature. That had to be it. No other explanation was possible.

I shook my head and blinked. Could I ask Omar? He had told me not to look—and it had just been my imagination anyway. "Uh, thanks, Omar," I said. "Gee, that feels better. I didn't like being reversed."

"Have to go back now," Omar said. He hurried across the lawn and pulled open the door. The music burst forth again.

"What's that music?" I asked him.

"Opera. Mr. Campanelli loves opera," he said, backing inside. "It's from *Hansel and Gretel,* by Humperdinck. It's called 'The Father's Song.' "

As I ran home I wondered if I ever wanted to go into 4-space again. I had only been there twice, and already it was causing me more trouble than I had bargained for.

# 8

But by the following Friday afternoon I was ready to go out there again. 4-space was scary, but I couldn't resist it. I wanted to learn how to get around in the other dimension, to be able to put the different views together so I would know where I was. Then I would be able to do all the wonderful tricks Omar could do. Then I would have the control and power I had imagined when Omar first told me about 4-space.

I might even be able to use that power to fix things with Pete. There would be plenty I could do to impress him if I could learn how to get into 4-space on my own.

Of course I didn't tell that to Omar. But he still refused to take me into 4-space. "I'm on duty this aft— I mean, I'm too busy," he said. "I have things to do."

I had noticed before that on some days he would be in a tearing hurry to get home. "What things?" I asked him.

"Oh . . . things," he said, walking faster. "Like, um . . . helping Mr. Campanelli . . . fight those highway people. They're pushing for that interchange again. Can't let them tear our houses down." He was moving ahead of me now. In the mornings, on the way to school, he always walked slower than I did.

"Come on, Omar. You're just trying to get out of taking me, aren't you?"

"I . . . It was a mistake to take you there, Laura." He looked away from me. "We really shouldn't go again."

"But I thought you liked sharing it with me, Omar. I thought you cared about me," I said, sounding hurt. "Pete will probably ask someone else to the dance, you know. A lot of the kids are starting to think I'm weird now, because of you. But I'm still your friend."

"But . . . you don't know how dangerous it is. I mean, if we get caught, they'd have to . . . kill us."

"But I'm not afraid, with you," I said, really laying it on. "It's our secret place that we have together. It's something no one else can give me—not even Pete. Don't you see what it means to me to go out there with you?"

He turned back to me, looking shyly up into my eyes. "You mean that, Laura?"

There was something about his expression that made me feel ashamed. I forced myself not to look away. "I mean it, Omar."

He sighed. "All right, all right. But I just *can't* today. I'm already late for . . ." His voice trailed off.

"Then tomorrow," I pleaded. "Take me tomorrow."

"Well, I'm off tomorrow—I mean, I'm not busy then."

"Off *what*, Omar?"

"I'll take you tomorrow, Laura, okay? I'll come over to your house. Now I have to go."

"Thank you!" I called after him.

The next morning he showed up early with all his equipment stowed in a book bag so nobody else would see it.

"I better go out by myself and check it out first," he said, up in my room. "To be sure nobody catches—I mean, nobody notices us."

I could hardly argue with that precaution. "Makes sense. Go ahead. I'll be waiting right here."

Omar rippled off by himself with his flashlight and gear, returning a few minutes later. "Looks like the coast is clear," he said, reaching for my hand. "Let's go."

"Try to remember not to bring me back reversed, okay?"

"I'll try." He closed his eyes and gritted his teeth. We jumped.

I kept my eyes open, fixed on Omar, to try to see what he did to pull us out there. But too much happened at once. The room swung away behind him so quickly that everything blurred. Omar flattened and smeared off to the side. A thick dark curtain of pipes and wiring and spiderwebs rushed past. Mice scurried. Omar's flashlight beam raked across a metallic, foam-filled bag with ⊤υO ƎbiƧ ꙅiʜT printed on it.

We landed. The movement stopped. The light fixture, which usually hung from the ceiling, now stuck out horizontally from the right, the little bugs still crawling around inside it. Omar hung between me and the light. His features were all pushed over to one side, like a modern painting in which you see the profile and the front view at the same time. A large part of what should have been his head was a mass of dark purple, penetrated by two sharp little beams of light.

"Omar," I whispered. "I think I'm looking inside your head."

He blinked, and the two little beams of light went off and on again. "Want to see it better?" he asked me, and moved his flashlight.

The dark purple blossomed into bright pinkish gray. A skull with squashed-together features grinned at me, surrounding a big soft wrinkled mess of brains.

"Thanks, Omar. Some other time." The light went out, the skull and brains vanished. "Where are we, exactly?" I asked him. "I want to start learning to find my way around."

"Try to figure it out. Look at where familiar things are. I can't do it for you."

I tried to concentrate. "Well, if the light fixture's hanging from the right, then . . . we must be standing on the wall of my room."

"That's it."

I struggled against dizziness. "But what about gravity? I . . . I don't *feel* weightless."

"We're not weightless. We're in 4-space gravity now. It goes perpendicular to all our 3-space directions."

"I don't get it. How can we be perpendicular to everything?"

"Think of the piece of paper. If we were flat creatures, we'd be standing with our feet on the paper, and the rest of us going *up* from the paper, at right angles to everything else. But it's not really up or down to us. It's *ana* or *kata.*"

I tried to imagine two flat creatures inside a line drawing of a house, sticking up from the page like cutouts. "Then . . . we should be able to take one step and be *outside* the house," I murmured.

"Right. Like this." Omar pulled me in a direction that, even on this third trip, I wouldn't have predicted. Pipes and stucco and clouds and tree branches zoomed around. Then I could see part of my room, veering off below. Two tilted dogs barked up from the snowy sidewalk hanging to the left. The winter sky stretched up on my right. We seemed to be standing sideways on the outside wall of the house.

I groaned. "I'm going to get used to this if it kills me!"

And over the next few days, I continued to beg and prod and wheedle Omar, and he continued, reluctantly, to give in and take me out there. He was my guide and instructor, and I had to admit that he was good at it. He was patient. He let me go at my own pace. And though he obviously loved to show off, he tried not to lecture *too* much, often not even answering my questions. "You have to figure it out for yourself," he would say. That could be infuriating. But it was also the best way to learn.

He would never even begin to hint at the technical side of getting into 4-space.

"But wouldn't it be easier if you showed me how to get there on my own?" I asked him. "Then you wouldn't have to drag me around all the time."

"You're not very heavy."

"Yeah, but . . . Why don't you trust me, Omar? When did I ever let you down?"

"That's not the point. You don't understand the risks, Laura. Anybody who gets caught out there has to die."

"Who says? You can't expect me to believe something like that if you won't explain."

But he wouldn't say any more. As timid as Omar was, he could be relentlessly stubborn. He still wouldn't let me enter his house or tell me anything about his home life. And I was getting more and more curious about *him*, not just about 4-space. Once I had pretended to be hurt by his reluctance to confide in me. But I wasn't so sure it was an act anymore.

I was actually beginning to like Omar, much to my surprise. He was gentler than any other boys I knew, and more patient. And I couldn't help but respect him for his sheer guts and courage—as well as competence—in 4-space. It was fun out there with him sometimes. We would laugh together and I would forget that he lisped and was plump and short, and was considered to be a jerk. And even though he wouldn't tell me everything, he really did seem to care about me and to understand how I felt.

And it wasn't just me he cared about. I began to see that there was a fundamental *goodness* about him. I was amazed by his attitude toward the kids at school, who treated him as an inferior without really knowing anything about him. "Don't you ever want to *show* them?" I asked him once.

"You know I can't let anyone else find out about 4-space," he said. "You wouldn't ever tell, would you?"

"No, no, that isn't it. What I mean is, I know the boys make fun of you in gym class. There must be some kind of trick you could do to make *them* look stupid for once when they start teasing you."

"It wouldn't change anything, Laura," he said. "That's just what kids are like. They want to be the same as everybody else." He shrugged. "Anyway, I don't need to do that to make myself feel big. Why hurt anybody if you don't have to?"

"Not even Pete?" I dared to say. I knew Pete was one of the ones who put Omar down—and Omar was also jealous of him, because by now Omar knew how I felt about Pete.

"Well, in *his* case, sometimes I'm tempted," Omar said, with a flicker of a smile. Then he added quickly, "No, but seriously, Laura, what would be the point? Anyway, he's a friend of yours."

I couldn't imagine Pete being that selfless in the same situation. And sometimes I even wondered why I did care about Pete so much. Omar was obviously a better person. Why couldn't I just forget about Pete and enjoy being with Omar?

But it wasn't so easy to keep feeling that way at school, where everybody looked up to Pete and looked down at Omar. However *good* Omar might be, there was still the real world to deal with. And the way to make it in the real world was to impress people like Arlene and go out with someone like Pete.

For about a week after the incident in the cafeteria, Pete didn't call me up and barely said more than "Hi" to me at school. Arlene told me he hadn't asked her out, but she made it clear that if he did, she would accept. Then one night he phoned me.

"Oh, hi," I said. "I'm so glad you called."

"You are? You weren't hoping it was Omar?"

"Oh, come on. How could I feel that way about Omar? I just get stuck with him all the time because he lives next door and doesn't have any other friends."

"Well that's very sweet and kind of you, Laura, but do you know what it looks like? It's kind of humiliating to have people think you'd rather be with a fat little jerk like that than with me."

"They'd have to be crazy to think that," I said heatedly. "Anyway, it won't be long now before . . . well, before I won't have to spend so much time with him." I was dying to tell him that by then I'd be able to get test answers ahead of time, that I'd be able to get us into sports events and rock concerts for free. But I knew it would sound crazy to say those things now, before I could actually do it. "Trust me, Pete. Just a little while longer. I know we can have a lot of fun together."

"Yeah? Maybe I was starting to think the same thing, *before* you started hanging around with Omar. But I can't just sit around waiting, Laura. And I *won't* keep being manipulated and put down by you."

"But I'm *not*, Pete." I didn't think I was manipulating him; I just wasn't doing things exactly the way *he* wanted. But I checked my impulse to argue. "Pete, believe me, we're going to have some *amazing* times together, soon, if you still want to."

"Yeah, Laura? Sure you're not just stringing me along?"

"I don't string people along."

"We'll see."

After that, I was more determined than ever to learn the trick of getting into 4-space on my own.

At the beginning I had been very clumsy. The first time I stepped *ana* across the wall into the bathroom, I kicked everything out of the medicine cabinet. The first time I pulled Omar *kata* over the ceiling into the attic, we got tangled up inside a bag full of old coats and mothballs. And once, I landed us inside the clothes dryer. Omar had kept his head and got us out of there before Dad opened the door.

But now I was acclimated out there. When I turned my head, I could predict what I was going to see next. Equipped with my own pocket flashlight, I could reach wherever I wanted. I learned the complicated routes of the pipes in the walls, so that I could confidently sip water from the pipe that fed the sink without being afraid I was drinking from the wrong pipe.

And every once in a while we would stumble into that other world, the place of shifting fragmented shapes where we had seen the 4-space creature on my first trip. I recognized it because of the bluish light and the utter unearthliness of everything. The actual landscape was never the same from one trip to the next. Once, we found ourselves awash in a sea of yellow tentacles that puffed up into fat balloons and then shrank down to spaghetti and puffed up again. We watched an endless train of undulating brown pyramids rush past us. And we caught a glimpse of another 4-space creature, four spheres of pink fur that rushed together into a fat fuzzy mattress, pulsing with static electricity, from which suddenly sprouted a fierce blossom of curving fangs.

We never stayed for more than a second or two. Omar always got us out of there fast. "But where *is* that place?" I asked him.

"That's the real 4-D world, all around our space. If our 3-D world was like the surface of a pool, then out there would be everything above and below the flat surface. Like I've told you, Laura. It's not *actually* above and below, it's the fourth direction, at right angles to our space. *Ana* and *kata*. The directions in 4-space that are on one side or the other side of us."

"But it's so weird and . . . *senseless* out there."

"It only looks that way because all we can see is cross sections of everything."

"I don't get it."

We had just come back from a trip. "Okay, Laura," he said. "Think of the flat surface of a pool. The flat 2-D people that live there can only see what's right on the actual surface of the water. They can't see anything above or below it. Now, what if a 3-D person dived into the pool with his hands stretched over his head? What would it look like to them?"

"Well . . . First they'd see ten fingers going into the water, I guess. They'd look like flat circles to them—the cross sections that cut through the surface."

"Circles of pink flesh," Omar put in. "What about when the rest went through?"

"Well, at the palms the circles would join together into two long ovals, and they'd shrink at the wrists, and then get bigger as the arms went through. And when the head hit the water, a circle would appear in between the two ovals—a hairy circle. When the face went through, some of the hair would go away and they'd see two eyes on the middle circle, and then a nose and a mouth. And when the shoulders went through, it would look like the three circles joined together into one long shape."

"Do you think they'd be able to make any sense of it?" Omar asked me. "It would look pretty weird, things splitting apart and joining together again."

"I guess it would."

"Well, that's how 4-space creatures look to us. We're like the flat people on the surface. We can only see the cross section passing through. Except that it's one dimension higher. Instead of seeing flat cross sections, we see solid spheres and blobs and things. That's all. Make sense?"

"Yes, but . . . it's kind of impossible to imagine what the whole creature would look like, if *slices* of it are like whole solid blobs." The idea made me a little queasy. "They must be even *more* hideous than what we've already seen." I dropped my voice, suddenly wondering if they could hear us. "What . . . what do their faces look like, Omar?"

"If you're lucky, Laura, you'll never know."

One night I set the table, just as usual. But Mom gave me a puzzled look when she came in with the salad. "Okay, Laura, very funny," she said, putting down the bowl. "Now do it right. Then call Dad."

"Huh?" I said. "Do *what* right?"

She frowned at me. "The table. Fix it."

"But what's the matter with it?" I looked at the table, genuinely puzzled.

She gestured impatiently. "Come on, Laura. Supper will get cold." She marched back into the kitchen.

I studied the table again. The knives and spoons were on one side of the plates, the forks on the other. I had put Dad on the end, Mom across from him, and me on one side. I really didn't see what was wrong with it.

But obviously something was. I had a sudden thought, and bent over and sniffed at a glass of water. It smelled like leftover tuna-fish salad. Meaning I must be reversed.

And I hadn't noticed.

My stomach went cold. I glanced around the dining room, at the windows on one wall and the door to the kitchen on the other. It *had* to be backwards. But I couldn't tell.

Last time it had been strikingly obvious. Everything had looked as though it were in the wrong place, and I had barely been able to find my way around the house. Now it didn't make any difference to me. The house looked perfectly ordinary.

I did my best to fix the table, then told Mom I felt sick, and went up to my room. It was true that I wasn't hungry. I was also in no mood to barge in on Omar, knowing he didn't want me there, and beg him to reverse me again. I figured I could get through the night without eating or drinking much.

More than anything else, though, I was scared. I had been so thrilled that I was getting the hang of moving around in 4-space. But in the process, I seemed to have lost something basic—my knowledge of left and right. What did that mean? Would I ever get it back?

And what other effects was 4-space having on me?

# 9

"And you didn't even notice?" Omar said. "Gee, Laura, you're . . . really making progress." He didn't sound thrilled about it.

We were on our way to school. Nothing looked peculiar to me at all—even though the sun was rising out of the west. "Why is it progress to forget the difference between left and right?" I asked him.

"Because it's a trivial difference. Left and right *kata* here— or *ana* here—doesn't matter much in 4-space. Sometimes you're looking at our world from *kata*, sometimes from *ana*. After you get used to looking at it both ways, you stop noticing the difference. Take a look at one of your books."

I stopped on the sidewalk and looked through my biology book. "It looks normal," I said. "But it *can't* be, Omar! It should be mirror writing, like the other time I was reversed."

"It *is* mirror writing, in relation to you. You can read both ways now. Congratulations. You've passed a big hurdle." He looked sick as he said it.

"Uh . . . thanks," I said distractedly. I wasn't sure I liked what had happened or what other implications it had.

I wasn't thinking very clearly as we hurried into biology. Before Mr. Dixon brought the class to order, he called Omar up to his desk, spoke quickly to him and gave him a note. Omar read it, frowning. Then he hurried out of the room.

Omar didn't come back during biology. After class, I made a point of leaving the room at the same time as Pete, so that we could walk to English together. Since our last phone conversation, when I had promised him that soon we would have some amazing times together, he had spoken to me a couple of times at school. His manner had been a little stiffer than it had been before the cafeteria incident, as though he was still nursing his wounded vanity, but at least he wasn't ignoring me. Today, with Omar away, I tried to be as charming as possible, smiling a lot and cracking jokes. Pete smiled a little, but he also kept watching my face in a speculative way, as though he wasn't sure he could trust me. It was frustrating, because I couldn't explain to him the real reason why I had been hanging around with Omar without giving Omar's secret away. I was going to have to find some other way to convince Pete that I really was interested in him.

In English, Mrs. Bowers called on Pete to diagram a sentence on the board. He did it badly, and she spoke sharply to him. When he went back to his seat, his face was flushed and petulant, just as it had been that day in the cafeteria. Then she called on me to diagram the same sentence.

I knew Pete would resent me if I did it right and showed him up in front of the class. So I did it wrong on purpose, forgetting I was reversed. Naturally no one noticed the mistake I made, because the sentence came out in mirror writing. The class, especially Pete, thought it was hilarious. Mrs. Bowers did not.

I hurried out of class to find Omar. I had to get him to reverse me back before anything else went wrong. I was also getting terribly hungry. I hadn't had supper the night before, and I was apprehensive about what reversed food—especially reversed school-cafeteria food— was going to taste like.

But Omar wasn't at his locker, and he wasn't in our next class. Then I remembered that Mr. Dixon had given him a note. I dashed in to ask Mr. Dixon about it before lunch. Omar, it seemed, had been called home because of some kind of emergency.

I felt like groaning. Just my luck, to end up reversed at school with Omar not there to flip me over. Who knew what kind of embarrassing thing would happen next?

Still, it gave me the chance to spend some time with Pete. And luckily there was an empty space at his table at lunch. "Okay if I sit here?" I said.

He shrugged. "Why not?" Then he smiled, more warmly than he had back in the corridor, almost as though he couldn't help it. "Hey, that was a pretty funny trick you pulled in English," he said. "That hag Bowers didn't know what to make of it."

"Oh, yeah," I said, thinking fast. I wanted to take advantage of what had happened, to help win Pete over again. "I just thought, diagramming sentences is such a stupid waste of time, and she's so serious about it. Why not shake her up a little, lighten things up?"

"That class sure needed it." Pete studied my face pleasantly. "You look different today, Laura. Softer around the eyes. You change your makeup or something?"

"Uh, yeah," I said, realizing that the way he saw me now was the way I usually saw myself in the mirror. "I'm starving," I said, to change the subject. "Good thing they're having hamburgers today. Not much they can do to ruin a burger."

"I wouldn't be too sure about that," said Arlene.

I tried to be as inconspicuous as possible about carefully smelling everything before tasting. The hamburger bun smelled like nail polish remover, so I pushed that aside. The meat itself didn't have much smell, so I took a cautious nibble. A mistake—it tasted exactly like the odor of dirty gym socks.

"I guess you were right, Arlene," I said lightly. "This place can make even a burger taste like dirty laundry."

"Dirty laundry. I thought I recognized the smell," Pete said, chuckling.

"I bet the cafeteria cooks raid the Lost-and-Found to find things from the locker room to stretch out the hamburger," I said, inspired by his approval. "It's probably one of the trade secrets they learn when they go to cafeteria-cook school. I was wondering what happened to those old sweatpants I lost."

"Cafeteria-cook school! I love it," Pete said.

I was still ravenous, and made a stab at the coleslaw. Another mistake. It not only smelled like fancy perfume, but it also *tasted* like fancy perfume, filling my mouth with a stinging soapy flavor. I had to kill the taste, and without thinking, I dipped a french fry in ketchup and bit into it.

The french fry turned out to be like a combination of anchovies and licorice, phenomenally repulsive in the same mouthful. But the ketchup—the ketchup! It was the most exquisitely delectable substance I had ever tasted. It was irresistible, as dark and luscious as the most expensive chocolate, as creamy and buttery as the richest frozen custard, with an unexpected tangy splash of freshly picked wild strawberries. In seconds I had slurped up the contents of the little plastic ketchup packet.

"You want your ketchup?" I said, reaching hungrily for the unopened packet on Arlene's tray.

"Not as much as you do, apparently," she said.

I ripped it open and squeezed it into my mouth. "I'll get you some more, be back in a sec," I said, jumping up and racing for the condiment table. I stuffed a half-dozen packets into my pockets, then returned with two big handfuls of them. I dropped one on Arlene's plate and tore open another.

Pete emptied a packet on his plate, stuck his finger in and licked it. "Just tastes like plain old ketchup to me," he said matter-of-factly, but still amused.

"Oh, if only you could really *understand!*" A tremendous idea occurred to me. All I had to do was go out into 4-space with some ketchup, reverse myself, and bring it back. Then it would be reversed ketchup. It would taste as incredibly delicious to everybody else as it did to me now. "I'll *prove* it to you," I said, grinning at Pete, feeling strangely light-headed all of a sudden. "Just you wait. I'll give you some ketchup that will *change your life!*"

Pete threw back his head and laughed. "Hey, Laura," he said. "How come you always used to seem so serious? I never knew you could be such a laugh riot."

"I told you you'd see my crazy side one of these days." I reached over and squeezed his chin between two fingers. "But you ain't seen nothin' yet. I have talents you wouldn't believe."

"Yeah?" Pete said, his eyes fixed on me. Then, abruptly, he stood up and looked at his watch. "You finished? Come on, we've still got a little time before next period. I want to show you something."

"Okay." I got up, lurching only slightly, and we started across the cafeteria. The entire room looked like a living stained-glass window, flooded with brilliant light and color, populated by angels. I sailed through them, smiling and waving blissfully at everyone I knew and a lot of people I didn't know.

The most beautiful angel of all was right beside me, impressed by my cleverness and wit. And the glorious taste of reversed ketchup still tingled on my tongue. The stuff didn't merely taste marvelous; it also made you *feel* so marvelous, in a totally unexpected way.

"By the way, where we going?" I asked Pete outside the cafeteria.

"To my secret place." He grinned at me and took my hand. We hurried up two flights of stairs, to the top floor of the building, then through a doorway and up a short flight of metal stairs I had never noticed before.

"Pete, where you taking me?"

"You'll see."

There was only a narrow space at the top, and a metal door. Pete turned the knob, leaned against the door to push it open, and stepped out into bright sunlight. "The roof," he announced. "Come on."

I followed him, wrapping my arms around myself. It was cold out, and we didn't have our coats. "I bet we're not supposed to be here," I said.

"Who's going to notice us? Nobody comes up here. I've been sneaking out here all year." He bent over and placed a pebble against the door frame, then carefully positioned the door against the pebble, to keep it open. The door was heavy and seemed to be the type that slams shut on its own. He stood up and guided me out onto the roof, his hand on my shoulder. "Look around. Isn't it great up here?"

The roof was flat, and since the school was at the top of a hill, you could see for miles. "Kind of cold. But yeah, it's beautiful," I said and giggled, still feeling the ketchup. "See that cloud? Looks just like a face. See the nose?"

"Uh huh," Pete said, not looking. He led me around to the other side of the little structure that enclosed the stairway, then pushed me gently against the wall, and did not take his hands away. "You like to dance?" he asked me, his breath sending little puffs of steam against my face.

"I love it! I'm a fantastic dancer," I lied happily.

"Well . . ." He paused, his face close to mine. "Would you like to go to the spring dance with me?"

"Yes," I said instantly.

"Good. Then it's a date." He put both arms around me and began kissing me.

Part of me knew it wasn't the time or the place. But under the influence of the ketchup, I had no resistance. Anyway, this was Pete, the best-looking, most popular boy in our class.

A minute or so later we noticed the bell, ringing distantly below us. Pete stepped away and looked at his watch. "Gee, I forgot about the time," he said, looking half-awake. "Got to get to gym. Come on."

The metal door was closed. "Huh?" Pete said. "But I put that pebble . . ." He pulled the handle. The door didn't move. "Oh, no," he whispered. "This doesn't . . ." He tried the door again. Then he groaned and turned toward me. "It's locked. The pebble must have slipped out."

I was too light-headed to feel much concern. "Well, at least there's a good view. And we have plenty of ketchup to eat."

"It's not funny, Laura." Pete shook the door again, then banged on it. "Hey, let us in! We're locked out!" he shouted.

We waited, listening. There was no response.

"Wouldn't it be a drag if we were stuck up here all night?" I said, and giggled again. "We'd probably freeze to death. My fingers are already numb."

"Don't say that, Laura! I've got to get to gym next period."

"Hey, I have a French test next period myself," I said. "Think she'd flunk me if I didn't show up?"

"But I can't miss gym!" Pete kicked the door. "Hey, we're locked out up here!" he shouted.

"Too bad Omar isn't here," I murmured. "He could just pull

us . . ." Then something occurred to me, and in my present state of mind it seemed to make sense. I was technically accomplished now. I didn't know left from right. I could read backwards and forwards. Maybe I didn't need Omar to pull me out there anymore. Maybe I *could* do it on my own.

"Omar? What's *that* jerk got to do with this?"

"Uh, nothing. Forget Omar," I mumbled, thinking hard. After all, I had made the trip with Omar over and over again. Moving *ana* and *kata* had become so natural to me that it had changed my brain. I knew what it felt like to move *ana* and *kata;* I knew where those directions lay. So why couldn't I just take a little step in one of those directions by myself? And what could I lose by trying?

If it hadn't been for the ketchup, I might have seen the trouble this could get me into. But I wasn't thinking about that. I stood still and closed my eyes. I concentrated hard. I thought about exactly what it felt like to move *ana* and *kata.* I pointed myself in the *ana* direction. I took a step.

But it was different from moving that way when I was already out there. It required a lot more sheer physical effort. It was like swimming straight down underwater, fighting the natural buoyancy that wants to pull you to the surface; like playing a tough game of tug-of-war or arm wrestling a strong opponent. I struggled, getting out of breath. I could feel the *ana* direction, I knew exactly where it was. I just had to push hard enough to get there.

"What's the matter with you, Laura? You look sick. Don't get hysterical now!" Pete said hysterically.

I fought harder, grunting, pushing *ana* with all my strength.

The pebbled roof dropped away. Pete shouted. I keeled over. The world bent and twisted and tilted off to the side. Then I was crouching on the wall, looking sideways down the stairs.

"Laura!" I heard Pete wail. "This can't . . . I don't . . ."

"Hey, pretty good!" I gasped. I had done it! I could hardly

believe it. I wanted to jump up and down and shout. 4-space belonged to me now.

"No. . . . Oh, no," Pete was whimpering *kata* and behind me.

The second bell rang. I did my best to think rationally. Then I carefully turned around, reversing the ketchup in my pockets and unreversing myself. I stepped over the wall, pulled myself down *kata,* and was standing inside the door. I pushed it open. "Come on in, Pete," I said, feeling smug.

"Huh?" Pete stood there staring at me, his mouth open.

"Come on, you'll be late for *gym.*" I pulled him inside, and the door slammed behind him.

"Laura? Am I going crazy? It looked like . . . you *disappeared.* And now you're in here!"

"Oh," I said, suddenly realizing I was going to have to come up with an explanation. How could I do it without betraying Omar? "I . . . I've got to go now." I turned and ran down the steps.

I did badly on the French test, still feeling fuzzy-headed and wondering what I was going to tell Pete. I tried to get away quickly after school, but he was waiting for me at my locker. "Laura, how'd you *do* that?" he demanded, keeping step with me as I hurried across the schoolyard.

Now I knew how Omar had felt. Pete was just as pushy as I had been, and just as unwilling to accept the line about being good with locks. He had actually seen me ripple off into 4-space, after all. If I hadn't been high on reversed ketchup, I never would have done it. Now I was trapped. I held him off all the way to my house. But by then he was getting angry.

"Laura, I *know* what I saw!" he said outside my door. "I'm not leaving until you tell me how you did it."

"Maybe you better . . . come inside," I said, thinking of Omar next door. He would be devastated when he found out I had betrayed him. Was it possible that he had been watching from 4-space and knew about it already? No, I quickly assured myself. If he'd been watching us on the roof, he would have opened the door himself instead of letting me go into 4-space in front of Pete. Anyway, he had been called away from school. Maybe I was lucky, and he was downtown somewhere, helping Mr. Campanelli fight the highway commission. He probably didn't know what I had done. Could I keep him from finding out?

"Do you still want to go to the dance with me, Laura?" Pete asked me in the front hall.

"The dance . . . ? Oh, yeah, the dance. Sure I do."

"Then tell me what happened on the roof. Now. I swear I'll never talk to you again if you don't. I'm waiting."

But I still hesitated. I seemed to care about Omar a lot more than I had realized. The thought of hurting him was agonizing. On the other hand, I couldn't bear to lose Pete. And maybe I didn't have to. After all, if Omar were watching now, he'd certainly let me know and warn me to keep my mouth shut. That meant Omar *had* to be occupied somewhere else. If I told Pete now, Omar might never know. Then I wouldn't have to give anything up. And even if Omar did find out, there wasn't anything he could do to get back at me. We were equal now. 4-space belonged to me too. Why shouldn't I share it with Pete?

*Because it's too dangerous,* Omar would have said. *Because anybody who gets caught in 4-space has to be killed.*

I tried to dismiss that worry. It was so extreme, and Omar had never given me any evidence at all that it was true.

Still, I did feel nervous up in my room when I started telling Pete about 4-space. He was a lot slower than I had been about picking up the concepts. He kept arguing about small points and saying things like "I wouldn't believe any of this stuff if I hadn't seen you disappear like that." I had to repeat the paper-doll routine several times before he got the idea behind it. And as soon as he did, he began pressuring me to take him out there immediately. I couldn't come up with any good excuse not to. I felt a little guilty about Omar, but I was also eager to show off for Pete. What other girl could offer him this kind of adventure?

And what other girl could offer him reversed ketchup?

"How come the label's backwards?" he said. "You're not just stalling, are you?"

"No, I'm not." It was a little disappointing—even irritating —that it took Pete so long to understand things. "The label's backwards because it's reversed, like I was telling you. I flipped it over in 4-space. Try it."

He opened one of the packets and squeezed it into his mouth. Then he practically jumped out of his chair. "What *is* this stuff? Where did you get it? It's incredible! Can I have another one?"

"I *told* you what it was, Pete," I said patiently, getting up. I tossed him another packet and went over to the closet to get my rope and flashlight.

"Hey, you got any more of this?" he said, dropping the empty packet, his voice husky.

"No, that's it," I lied. I didn't want him to get out of control. And I wasn't foolish enough to eat any myself. One of us was going to have to have her wits about her where we were going.

"Hey, Laura, anybody ever tell you what a great mouth you have?" he said, lolling back in his chair and beaming up at me. He reached out and grabbed me around the waist.

"Not now!" I pulled away from him, knelt down and hurriedly tied one end of the rope around the leg of my desk. "If you want me to take you into 4-space you're going to have to do what I say," I told him. "It's confusing out there, and I don't have a whole lot of experience." Leaving the main body of the rope neatly coiled, I stood up and threaded the other end several times through one of my belt loops. "It could even be dangerous," I went on, "so you have to follow my instructions. Could you stand up, please?"

"Yes, ma'am," he said, standing up and smiling at me. I couldn't help smiling back, he looked so appealing, with his curly blond hair and dimpled chin. He had taken off his sweater, and was wearing a T-shirt that clung to the muscles on his upper arms and chest.

"What's with the rope?" he said.

"So we can find our way back." I tied the end of the rope securely around one of his belt loops, leaving a couple of feet in between us. I grasped the thick coil in my left hand. It was a fifty-foot length of clothesline, meaning there was at least forty feet between us and the desk. We certainly wouldn't want to go any farther away than a couple of steps from my room.

Tying the rope made me think of Omar again, and the first time he had taken me into 4-space. I felt a terrible pang. I knew this was going to wound him badly. And maybe it really *was* more dangerous than I realized—he might have had a good reason not to tell me any more than he had. But at least I hadn't said anything to Pete about Omar. He didn't know that Omar had anything to do with it at all.

"Come on, Laura. You're not going to back out now, are you?" Pete coaxed me, looking down at me with what seemed like real warmth in his wonderful blue eyes.

I took his hand. It was so much nicer than Omar's, cool and strong and dry. "Don't let go of my hand, no matter what," I said. "Here we go."

But moving *ana* was even harder with Pete in tow than it had been on my own. I felt for the direction, I leaned into it. But this time I was fighting against a thick web of invisible rubber cords that held us back. I pushed harder than I had before, gasping. The cords quivered against me, humming in their intensity to keep us back. I struggled against them.

And I felt them begin to weaken. I knew I could break through. I gritted my teeth, grunted, and wrenched myself *ana* with every muscle in my body.

The cords broke. Pete cried out as we burst through. Then we were tumbling over and over in the *ana* direction. Because of Pete's extra weight, I had been pushing too hard when the cords suddenly let go. Now I flailed wildly to slow our momentum as we rolled over and over each other, down what felt like a steep slope.

When we stopped rolling and I opened my eyes, I saw that we had gone a lot farther than one or two little steps from my room.

# 10

Bright red spiky shapes bobbed and swelled against us, changing like patterns in a kaleidoscope. Pete yelled.

But they weren't hurting us. Their touch was velvety and delicate. We lay against something cushiony. Where were we?

I turned my head. High above us—or perhaps it was *kata* from us, or below us, I wasn't sure—greenish tendrils expanded and shrank against a background bubbling with purple and orange. Was I looking at a sky? It seemed to be early morning or late afternoon here.

I hoped it was early morning.

"Laura?" Pete said faintly. "Do . . . do you see what I see? It's just the ketchup, right? Just a hallucination, isn't it?"

"Afraid not," I said. "This is real, Pete. The 4-space world, the world on either side of our space. Like I was trying to tell you."

"No, it's not," he moaned, and I could feel him trembling beside me. "It's not real. It's not, it's not."

"Shhh! Let me think. I've got to get my bearings."

I turned my head away from the sky. Everything changed completely. Now all I saw were textured columns, some tilted sideways, some hanging above and below us, branching and intertwining, fading into the distance in all directions. I looked down at my hand, muscle and bone and skin on a blue mat surrounded by brown gnarled lumps. A black speck appeared out of nowhere, ballooned into a fuzzy ball, grew scurrying legs and vanished—even before I had time to whip my hand away and shout.

In the distance, something shrieked back. Wind rustled.

My gaze shifted. More tunnels formed by rough columns, darker. A group of feathery puffs, expanding, contracting, sprouting eyes and cartilage, cackling, shrinking away to nothing.

I closed my eyes and groaned.

"What were those things? Why did they do that? Did you *see* that?"

"They're just cross sections," I told him. "They're not really doing that. It just looks that way, because you can only see parts of them moving past your surface. Like I was trying to explain to you before."

"I don't get it," Pete whined, turning toward me. Then he gulped, deep in his throat. I didn't blame him. All the way out here in 4-space, fully illuminated by 4-space light, we could see inside of each other without the aid of a flashlight. From one specific angle, Pete looked normal. Then he moved a little, and part of his liver would peek out around the edge, a section of his lungs, and then all the rest. The sight of all those living, slimy, bloody organs—not to mention such substances as flowing mucus and half-digested food—was a lot more intense than a little dead frog in biology class. "Laura . . . I can see . . . inside . . ."

"Then don't look," I said, turning away from him. "Just don't look at me, till you get used to it. At least we *can't* see inside 4-space things."

"But I don't like this. Kill it. Don't you have a pill to make it go away?"

"I told you, this isn't like that. It's real." We had to get back to my room as fast as possible. Thank God we had the rope to show us the way. It was so complicated here that I had lost any sense of which direction we had rolled from.

The rope was tangled all around us. I stood up and got Pete to his feet. He waited there numbly with his eyes shut as I managed to unwrap the rope from him and then from myself, trying to look at him as little as possible. Almost the entire length of it seemed to have come uncoiled as we fell. I began pulling it in and coiling it up again, expecting at any moment to feel the reassuring tug as it tightened, tied to my desk on the other end.

But it didn't tighten. I kept coiling. And then there was no more rope to coil. I felt the end of it in my hand.

In our fall, the hasty knot I had tied had come loose. The rope was not attached to the desk.

"No!" I screamed. How far had we gone? I turned in a frantic circle, searching for my room. The tilting avenues of columns billowed and rolled like curtains in a breeze. The sky, more purple now, blinked on and off, tiny lights like fireflies racing across it, dark green tendrils inflating and dancing and shriveling into spikes, red pointed petals bursting open and shrinking away.

And nowhere a glimpse of lamp or bookcase or stucco wall or blue afternoon sky.

"What's the matter?" Pete was whispering. "Why did you scream? What's happening?"

"The rope. It came untied from my desk. We . . . we can't use it to get back."

"You still talking about getting back somewhere?"

I knew he had eaten the ketchup, but I was still irritated by his inability to understand. "Pete, we are in another *dimension*," I said in a furious, singsong voice, as though talking to an infant. "The rope was the way back to my *room*. The rope came *untied*. Now we don't *know* the way back. Do you get it now?"

"Came untied . . ." he muttered. "Another . . ." Then his voice changed. "You let the rope come untied? How could you be so *stupid*?"

"Just shut up and let me think!"

I tried desperately to be logical and not give in to hysteria. I didn't know how far we had tumbled out of 3-space. But we had rolled far enough so that there were now solid 4-space objects between us and our thin sliver of a world—a world that we would probably only be able to see from certain specific spots in 4-space. One of those spots might not be very far from where we stood. But we could find it only by going in exactly the right direction. And there were so many directions here. Every inch we moved in a wrong direction would make our chances of getting home even more hopeless.

I didn't know what to do. I didn't dare to move. We could not risk going the wrong way and losing ourselves forever. We probably already were lost forever.

A wail threatened to tear itself out of my throat. I clenched my teeth and pressed my hand over my mouth to stifle it. We were fragile paper dolls in a sudden and violent world. We must not draw attention to ourselves.

Why hadn't Omar told me how hard you had to push to get here and how suddenly the bonds of 3-space let go, flinging you out? If I had known how easy it was to get lost, I wouldn't have tried it on my own. Why hadn't he warned me?

But that wasn't fair. Omar had told me it was dangerous. And he hadn't thought I'd do anything as stupid as going into 4-space without him. This was my own fault.

I could no longer pretend it might be morning here. The bewildering shapes all around us were fading more quickly into dim twilight. In a way, it was a relief not to see the constant lunatic changes so clearly, not to see Pete's brains every time I looked at him. The darkness was forbidding. But it also made us less conspicious and, perhaps, less vulnerable.

And back in 3-space, it was still mid-afternoon. As the night deepened here, we might be able to see a glow from wherever 3-space was, a glow that would have been invisible in bright daylight. Maybe we did have a chance. Meanwhile, where were we?

It was definitely a sky up there. And the inflating and shrinking tendrils might be cross sections of branches and leaves. The black scurrying thing could have been an insect, the feathery things birds. But what about the textured columns forming tunnels in all directions?

Trees. We had rolled into some 4-space woods or forest.

The darker it got and the less everything appeared to expand and contract, the more ordinary the view became. I was looking at stars, flickering on and off as foliage swayed and trembled around us. I heard distant chirpings and whistling calls, the soft brushing hiss of trees in the wind.

Pete and I were still holding hands. "Pete, you've got to look around," I told him firmly. "Try to get a feel for this place. That's the only way we'll ever be able to get out. We're in some kind of forest, I think."

"But why does it look like this?" he whimpered, frightened again. "Why does everything keep changing?"

"Because we're in 4-space. And our eyes can only see three-dimensional sections of it. So every time something moves, we see a different part of it—a different cross section."

This time I made an attempt to stifle my irritation at his helplessness and to remember how patient Omar had been with me. Disoriented as I was, it must be infinitely worse for him. "Do you remember what I told you back in my room, about the difference between a flat, two-dimensional world, and our three-dimensional world? And what our world would look like to a two-dimensional person?"

"How can you think about *geometry* at a time like this?"

"Because it's the only way to understand where we are! It's the only way we'll ever find our way home!" I pushed my hair away from my face and launched into the explanation Omar had given me of a person diving into a pool. "All I'm trying to say is, this place probably *isn't* as horrifying and dangerous as it looks to us. It's like being out in the woods, with one extra dimension. Or in a park." I squeezed his hand reassuringly. "Or maybe even just somebody's safe backyard."

Something howled hungrily in the distance. Something else roared back—something that sounded a lot more like a lion than a pet chihuahua.

"A park, Laura? It's a *jungle*! Those things sound *big*! You got us here. Now get us out!"

"I'll do what I can. But you have to help too, not just blame me and whimper and make everything worse!" With my free hand, I slapped dirt off my sweatshirt.

"I wasn't whimpering," he said sullenly. "Anyway, what about the rope? Didn't you notice where it was coming from when you reeled it in? That's where your room would be."

"I know that. But it's hard to remember exactly which direction it was. There's an extra direction out here, remember? Anyway . . . I think it might have been . . . over there, maybe."

I turned unsteadily in the darkness, trying to remember.

There was another howl, distinctly closer now.

"Well, let's *go* there then," he said, tugging at my hand, "before that *thing* gets to us."

"No, wait, stop!" I pulled him back. "Did it feel to you like we rolled fifty feet?"

"No. Less than that."

"Okay. That means that from *this exact spot*, the rope is long enough to reach back to my room. But if we go running off in the wrong direction and can't find our way back here, then we won't have any chance at all. So what we have to do is keep one end of the rope here, so we can always get back to this place, and then try out different directions, as far as the rope can go. That's the only way of making sure we'll get back."

"Oh," he said. It was too dark to see him, but I recognized that petulant edge to his voice that meant he resented me for being right. "Okay, then let's just tie it to a tree," he said.

"Or a root. I know I saw . . ." Then I remembered something Omar had told me. "The rope came untied, from both our belts."

"If you weren't so lousy at knots, we wouldn't be in this mess."

"You're full of it!" I said, kicking 4-space dirt at him. "I didn't tie a good knot to my desk because you were pawing at me. But I tied good knots around our belts. And they came untied. The only reason we didn't lose each other was because we were holding hands. Knots don't work in 4-space."

The animal howled again.

"What are you talking about?" Pete whispered. "Just let me tie it to a root so we can get out of here."

"I'm telling you, knots don't work in 4-space," I hissed. "They slip out, because of the extra direction. You *can* knot a plane, like a piece of paper. But you can't knot a rope."

"Just give it to me!"

"All right, go ahead, waste your time trying it," I said, uncoiling a couple of feet of rope and thrusting it at him. "But I'm looking for a rock to anchor it with."

I fell to my knees and groped around on the ground, holding the body of the rope with my left hand while Pete fumbled with the end of it, muttering, "Stupid thing! It's like spaghetti. Dumb kind of rope you picked."

"It's not the rope. It's the extra direction. Here's a rock." I tugged on the rope to pull him over. It wasn't easy to get a grasp on the rock until I realized I had to move my hands *ana* and *kata* to get them around it. "Uh . . . Okay, I've got one end up. Shove the rope underneath."

We managed to get the rope underneath it, then tugged on it sharply to make sure it was securely anchored. The animal was close enough now so that we could hear a deep rumbling purr through the trees, and padding footsteps.

"Hurry up," I whispered.

At least the direction I thought we might have come from was away from the animal noises. I started along a leafy tunnel that sloped upwards, *kata*, and to the left. I moved slowly, climbing, crawling sideways at times, feeling ahead before each step, carefully unreeling the rope behind me. Pete kept close to me, gripping my hand.

It was not completely dark. We could dimly see the trees around us in a greenish silvery light, dark shapes that swelled up and shrank away as we moved past them. Twisted branches sprang out unpredictably, like living things grabbing for us, startling me every time—and startling Pete even more. I had to keep telling him that they were only branches in cross section and that we had to move *ana* or *kata* to get around them, like moving over a wall back at home. Pete, who had no concept of *ana* and *kata* at all, had to be guided every inch of the way at first. It was going to take us forever to get to the

76

end of the rope—and it was pretty unlikely that this first stab was exactly the right direction. We would probably just have to struggle all the way back to the rock and start all over again.

The only thing we had going for us was that the animal noises seemed to be growing fainter. Perhaps it had not caught our scent. 4-space creatures might not even be aware of 3-space smells, I told myself hopefully, and might have no interest in eating us. After all, we'd be like paper dolls to them, and who eats paper dolls?

At one point I stopped and looked up and *ana*, raking my eyes back and forth across the sky. I saw a mottled green sphere, shrinking and expanding as I moved my head, and *kata* from that, a blue sphere. There were two moons here, and maybe more that hadn't risen yet.

I pointed them out to Pete, and we both just stood there and stared miserably at them. That was a bad moment, and I almost felt like giving up. What kind of alien place was this, with two moons? It must be incredibly far away. How could we ever hope to get home? I wanted to cry. I didn't want to be here.

I pulled myself together, and we moved on. Nightbirds cackled; the sighing of the leaves rose and fell like some immense creature drawing breath. Behind us a small animal skittered away through the foliage.

And something glittered between the trees, above us, *kata*, and to the right.

The glow of afternoon from 3-space? We rushed toward it. A tree branch reached out and punched me in the stomach. I gasped, stunned for a moment.

*Yesssss. Just a little more pruning, while the fool wastes his time in there, yessss, mine will be juicer, healthier. . . .*

Then I bent *kata* out of the branch's way and pulled Pete after me. I kept my eyes fixed on the glow above, moving slowly again, knowing that I could easily lose sight of the glow if some

4-space object got in between. But the trees thinned and the light increased as we approached it. It seemed to be in a clearing. Was it possible that we had already stumbled onto the way back home?

We reached the clearing. Disappointment slammed through me. I had no idea what the intersection of 3-space and 4-space should look like. But I suspected that it could not possibly be as small as this glowing object.

"Is this it? The way back?" Pete demanded.

"I think it's too small. And the light. It just doesn't look like sunlight from home."

"Don't be so negative!" Pete snapped. "Come on. Let's check it out."

"But . . ."

"Well, *I'm* going."

As we climbed into the clearing, we could see more clearly, in the glow, the ever-changing shapes of 4-space objects around us. The trees on the edge of the clearing appeared to sprout limbs that danced as we walked. There were growing things within the clearing as well, but they seemed to be arranged in some kind of complex though orderly pattern, and they were a lot smaller than the trees—small enough so that we could see over and *kata* them to the source of the light. We moved closer.

*Enough, enough, yesssss. Must hurry back now before the greedy old hog eats it all up himself. . . .* Giggling . . .

I froze. "Wait! Did you see that?"

"See what? Come on."

"That dark shape. Big. Like something moving away through the trees over there." I felt the beginnings of a nightmare panic. The movement—had I really seen it?—had been so hulking and strange. "And I just had the funniest feeling, Pete. Like a kind of voice. Inside my head."

"You're imagining things. Come on. I want a closer look."

Maybe it had been my imagination. And I wanted a closer look myself.

The glowing object sat upon a 4-space rock that bubbled and squirmed in typical 4-space style as we approached. So too did the source of light—a transparent, crystalline thing with a bright bluish flickering inside it—change its shape as we moved. For one moment it would be a simple, familiar cube. Then, as we took a step closer, an edge would split to reveal two more faces within; another step, and a corner would open out into a multifaceted star.

We walked slowly around it, scraping our shins on the growths that kept swelling out of the rock like granite balloons. And the glittering object on the rock would swallow itself up into an ordinary cube again and then unfold into a kind of diamond, deep rifts appearing as sparkling edges separated and subdivided into more sections, and once again would close together, shrinking accordionlike into a cube.

I glanced at Pete. Arlene probably wouldn't have found him very attractive at this moment, with his clogged sinuses and wrinkled brain and grinning skull, bluish in this light. But I thought I detected in his squashed-together eyes a real sense of wonder at what we were seeing, despite the terrible predicament we were in. Arrogant and stupid as he was, there might be a good side to him after all.

"*Amazing.*" He breathed. "This is like the most fantastic light show or . . . or computer graphics display anybody could ever imagine. What's it doing out here in the middle of the woods?"

"It's just an ordinary lantern," I said, unable to resist showing off that I knew more than he did. "Just a candle inside a glass box—except that the box happens to be a hypercube."

"A *what?*" he said, irritated.

"A hypercube—a 4-space cube. It's like if you take a two-dimensional square and stretch it out into the third dimension, it becomes a cube, a three-dimensional solid. And if you take a cube, and stretch it out into the fourth dimension, it turns into *this* thing—a four-dimensional solid. A hypercube."

"Bull!" he said. "An ordinary lantern doesn't—"

*Late again, lazy and irresponsible as always! You are fortunate I am so terribly terribly kind and have saved you a piece of the head. And do not blame me if it is tough, not to mention bloodless. . . .*

Pete choked and slapped his hands over his ears.

"You did feel it then! It's not my imagination."

"Did you hear . . . that voice?"

I could see Pete's purplish heart speeding up. "Something about saving something to eat?" I whispered. "Not words, exactly. Ideas. Inside my head."

He turned to nod at me, then looked quickly away, blood draining out of his face. He seemed to be more squeamish about people's insides than I was. "Yeah," he managed to mumble. "Something about . . . the food being tough."

We retraced our steps and walked back around the rock, unwrapping the rope from it. I kept my eyes on the lantern, which had a hypnotic fascination.

"Hey! Look over there!" Pete said, pointing.

"Which way?" There were too many directions for a single pointing skeletal hand to indicate them all.

"On the other side of the clearing, downward, to the left, and one of those other directions."

I looked *kata* from his hand, then *ana.* Another glimmer of light. But brighter, at this distance, than the lamp had been. And not blue, like the lamp, but pink. The pink of a 3-space sunset?

"Let's go!" Pete said.

"But . . ."

Pete rushed for it without waiting, pulling me by my right hand. The last loop of rope uncoiled and slid across my left palm. "Stop! The rope!"

Pete stopped so fast I crashed into him. I squeezed the rope in my fist just in time to keep it from slipping away.

"We reached the end?"

"Yeah. I got it just in time." I closed my eyes in relief. "I guess this is as far as we go."

"*What?*" Pete shouted.

"Shhh! They'll hear us."

"But that looks like our sky over there. We can't stop now. It could be the way back."

"It's too far," I said. "The rope doesn't reach it."

"Are you *totally* sure we didn't roll farther than the rope?"

*Tough and bloodless, you say? An understatement. My teeth cannot tell where the skull ends and the brains begin.*

*Thanks to you, for being so late. And what, by the way, were you doing out there? I can always tell when you're hiding something, mulish one. . . .*

"There it is again!"

"I know, I know." We were still close enough to the lantern so that I could see Pete's jaw tighten, and each individual tooth grind against another tooth. "But are you *sure* we didn't roll any farther than the length of rope?" he said.

"I thought I was sure." It wasn't easy to think clearly under the circumstances. "But . . . I guess it's possible we could have rolled farther."

"Then let's go check out that light. I bet it's the way back. I just have this feeling."

"And lose the rope?" I said, horrified. "Pete, it's our only connection to the place where we landed. If we leave the rope, and that light *isn't* the way home . . . Then we'll never find it again. We'll never get back, for sure!"

"Never find the rope again?" he said, a little smugly. "Think,

Laura. Just leave the end of the rope on that rock, where the lantern is. Then, if this isn't the way home, the lantern will show us where the rope is."

"Oh." He did have a point. But there was still something he hadn't thought of. "All right, but . . . if that pink light isn't the way home, then what is it? This lantern, those thoughts inside our heads. Maybe it's a house, Pete. Maybe somebody lives there."

"Yeah, maybe somebody does," he said, shrugging. "And then they can help us, show us the real way back if this isn't it. That's what you're supposed to do when you're lost in the woods, go for the light, not run away from it."

I remembered what Omar had said about having to be killed if you got caught in 4-space. It seemed a lot easier to believe at this moment then it had been back at home. "But this isn't just the woods, Pete," I said. "This is 4-space." Couldn't he understand? "You don't know what kind of creatures live here. I've seen them. They're *gross!*"

*Just as well for you you do not eat much, my toad-faced friend. You have been growing quite repulsively fat recently. Do not deceive yourself that I have not noticed it. . . .*

"*That* might be what lives there," I said, fighting to push the invading thoughts out of my mind. "It doesn't sound too friendly."

"We don't have to go barging in on it. Just close enough to see. And if it's not the way home and it looks dangerous, then we'll just come back here to the lantern and get the rope."

"But . . ." I didn't like his plan. Still, we did have to make sure that the pink light wasn't the way home. And the lantern *would* guide us back to the rope. "All right," I said.

We went back to the rock and carefully set the rope down on it. We hurried across the clearing in the direction of the light. We clambered downward, *ana,* and to the left, moving more quickly now that we were getting more accustomed to this place. The light ahead was already brighter and clearer, looking more and more like a sunset.

Then I turned briefly back—just in time to see the lantern flicker.

A bird shrieked. The lantern flickered again, faded, and went out. Silvery green dimness swallowed up the clearing and the rope. And, in only an instant, I lost my sense of where they had been.

## 11

"Hey, Pete? Look back at the lantern, where the rope is," I said.

"What for?" But he stopped and turned. Then he had nothing to say.

"Think you can find the rope now?" I asked, so furious at him I actually felt a certain satisfaction that his plan had backfired.

"We'll find it in the morning." He refused to admit he had made a mistake. "We'll be able to see the clearing then. And maybe this *is* the way back. Come on."

*I just think it is rather amusing that a blemish such as you would call me fat, that is all. Have you taken a thoughtful look at yourself recently?*

"God, I wish it would shut up!" I said as we squelched through mud toward the pink light. It was bad enough having these uninvited thoughts forced into our heads. Why did they also have to be so petty and bickering?

"Shhh," Pete said. We stopped and peered past a clump of shimmering shrubbery.

The oblong of pink light was quite close now, tilting away from us at yet another peculiar angle. But if the light was coming from a house, we could make out nothing of the building—focusing our eyes on the light had blinded us to whatever might be surrounding it.

"Come on," Pete whispered, pulling my hand.

"You want to go *closer?*"

"We'll be careful."

But Pete had never had a glimpse of real 4-space creatures, those slimy globs of flesh, constantly changing, wrenching apart and fusing together again, rolling along and suddenly growing mouths in unexpected places. "Pete. Listen to me. You have no idea what the creatures here are *like*. I told you, I've seen them. They're worse than you could ever think. And Omar said . . . they'd have to kill us if we got caught out here."

"Omar? What does he know about any of this? You're just being hysterical. This really might be the way home. We *have* to find out."

*I do not need to sit here and be abused and insulted by the likes of you. And I do not appreciate your references to my face, pitiless one. My poor face was changed by an accident and has nothing to do with overindulgence, as you well know.*

Against my will, we moved closer, doing our best to ignore the intrusive thoughts. Now there was no shrubbery, only a kind of thick, carpetlike mat beneath our feet. I was terrified. I felt pretty sure we hadn't fallen this far out of 3-space. And how could we have rolled past all those trees without being stopped by them?

Still, the closer we got to the light, the less it looked like a window, and the more it did look like a solid section of pink sky. And the smell of food cooking was achingly familiar. It would be suppertime at home. . . . Maybe all we had to do was reach the bottom of the oblong. I began to hope again. In another minute we might be tumbling into my room. They'd be amazed at how nice I'd be tonight. I'd set the table, I'd clear the table, I'd do all the dishes. And I'd be Omar's friend forever. I'd never bother him about 4-space again. He could have it.

And then an entire wall of pink light exploded in front of us.

# 12

*Ohhhh! What do I see?* A voice like many whispers echoing out of a cave. *And I almost trod upon them. . . . Ohhh, cunning creatures!*

Shadows swooped and swelled. A withered, veiny donut encircled me in a rush of velvet curtains, squeezing gently. I screamed, and squirmed in its grasp, and managed to get a glimpse of Pete, screaming too, surrounded by another gnarled inner-tube of flesh. My stomach dropped as we were lifted in a breathless rush—lifted past a snoutlike bloating mass that suddenly sank in upon itself into three deep, crusted pits. Pete blurred out of focus and vanished. And then a wrinkled beach ball of an eye swam toward me—yellow-veined, with a purple iris—an isolated globe independent of any face, hanging suspended in the dancing light.

We didn't seem to be at home.

*Trod upon what, elephant-legged one?*

The eye shrank to a point and vanished.

*They are mine! I found them first! They are mine, mine, MINE!*

The intensity of the voices inside my head numbed me to everything else. I thought of a story I had heard about a soldier forgetting he has a toothache when his leg is blown off. I could actually bear to watch as a pair of lips like writhing reptiles swept past, then a jutting prominence with sparse whiskers that brushed across my face, a sideways glimpse of hanging wattles like great swags and draperies of skin, and I was whisked down *ana* and around, and pressed against something like fabric.

*Show me! Show me what you have found! Take your hands from behind you.*

*They are mine. I will not let you take them from me!*

And there was Pete, close beside me again, his head poking out from between a grimy scimitar of fingernail and a ridge of folded knuckle. And even though I could see inside his head, it was still a relief to look at something that was *not* a shifting cross section, but an easily identifiable whole.

He looked sick.

*Did I say I would take them from you, insect-brain? I only said I wanted to see them.*

*I do not trust you.*

Trust him! Trust him! I felt like screaming. No wonder Pete looked sick. Aside from everything else, the creature's grip around our necks was not particularly gentle.

*Of course you can trust me. And in any case, you will have to show me sometime. So do it now.*

*What will you promise me if I do?*

"Pete!" I called out softly. "Pete, are you hurt or anything? Can you hear me?"

He coughed, and his eyes flickered open. "Laura?" he gasped. "Oh . . . you *are* there." He swallowed, with difficulty. "I'm choking. But the worst part is . . . I think I went psycho. Too much . . . to take."

"No, Pete. I tried to tell you: *This* is what they look like to us. See why I didn't want to get near them?"

*Why should I promise you anything? They are probably only a pair of brain-damaged field vermin.*

Laughter like serenading chainsaws. *No, no, Ramoom, they are marvelous and amazing. They are fantastic beyond your imagination. But they are also delicate, unearthly, easily vanishing. If I were to toss them outside, we might never find them. No, no, you must promise.*

"If you're trying to say 'I told you so,' you might as well shut up," Pete managed to say. "This is all your fault."

"Can't you see I'm just trying to *help* you, you jerk?" I shouted at him. "You're not crazy. If we could see all of them at once, they might not look that different from people."

*Promise what, then?*

*That you will not take them from me. That you will never, ever tell anyone else about them. And that . . . you will stay with me for another season.*

A sense of hesitation, doubt. *You ask many promises, Gigigi. I was expecting only one. Are they worth so much, then?*

*That is what I ask. Or you will never see them.*

Their conversation, though alien and voiceless, was beginning to sound somehow familiar.

*Do you promise?*

*Yes, yes, I promise!*

*You must take my hand.*

*All right, all right. Here, I take your hand.*

I wondered, vaguely, how that was possible, since this creature was still holding us with both hands behind its back.

*Let the promise be made, then. And now . . . behold them!*

More bewildering shapes rushing by. And then the blissful relief of being released, set down on some rough surface, Pete beside me. We both gasped, staggering a little. And then we fell toward one another, clinging together.

*No, no, do not blend and hide. Let Ramoom see you.*

We sprang away from each other before the gnarled blobs swimming toward us could push us apart—though I did not let go of Pete's hand.

*For once, Gigigi, you amaze me! All that you said about them was true. Incredible, gossamer creatures. They are indeed beings out of legend.*

Six spherical, disembodied eyes floated in the flickering light. They were arranged in two triangular groupings of three, each group containing one purple, one yellow, and one green iris. And I knew, from the conversation, that there were only two creatures here.

I pulled Pete's head over, so he'd see the same section of space. "You see what I see, Pete? Six eyes?"

"Uh-huh." He nodded miserably.

"I guess they're not very much like people after all."

*If I could not see them, I would not believe they could exist. Transparent creatures! I have never conceived of such a thing. Rather a primitive and peculiar anatomy, I must say—*

*Do not insult them! Do not hurt their feelings or I will take them away!*

*Primitive life forms do not have feelings, Gigigi, you ass. And you cannot deny that their anatomy is strange. You are over-protective of them, perhaps because of your own, shall we say, anatomical peculiarities. . . .*

*Do not keep insulting me, Ramoom. That is another promise you must make.*

I turned toward Pete. "God, I wish they'd stop bickering all the time."

*They are indeed evanescent, vanishing. We must keep them safe, so that they will not slip away, escape from us.*

*What do you mean by safe, Ramoom?*

One set of eyes shrank away and vanished. *Safe . . . ? The cage I made when you found that wounded bat you made such a stupid fuss about. I told you it would die. But perhaps making that cage was not such a waste of time after all.*

The other eyes were swallowed by a tangled gray mat, a cottage thatched with human hair that billowed into nowhere. *But to put them in a cage, like animals?*

*But they are animals, Gigigi, you sentimental fool.* Dim, blurred shapes ballooned and separated and fused in the distance amid crashes and thumps. *Ah, there it is.*

I stepped backwards into warm slime. I jumped away with a cry of disgust, slipped and fell, dragging Pete down with me.

*There you are in the head drippings! Hungry, is that it, my little ones?* And before we could do anything else we were pulled apart and lifted again.

*Quickly, Gigigi. In here!*

A click, a squeal of hinges, and we landed on fuzzy softness. A dark grid of diamond shapes changing to squares swung toward us and slammed with a jangling crash. Then we were swinging sickeningly. A moment later we felt a jolt, from *ana* and above us, and the swinging gradually diminished. And as we stabilized, there were the eyes again, hanging fascinated on the other side of the grid.

"Get us out of this thing, Laura, like you got us out off the roof. I can't stand those eyes watching me!"

There wasn't much point in leaving the cage now, with their full attention upon us. But I knew how he felt. Being trapped and closely observed was so unbearable that rationality vanished; all that mattered was getting away. I grabbed Pete's hand, and we stumbled across the cage to another wall of grid. I tried to move *ana* over the wall, then *kata*. But it wasn't like moving over a wall back at home. *Ana* and *kata* over this wall was only more solid grid. There was no way out. If I'd been thinking, I would have known it without even trying. I let go of Pete's hand and sank to my knees.

"Now what's the matter with you? I told you to get us out of here!"

"It's no use, Pete." Suddenly I felt too exhausted even to be angry at his stupid hostility. "We can't go out into 4-space to get out of this thing because we're already *in* 4-space. This isn't just a regular box, it's a hypercube, like that lantern. Every *surface* of this thing is a solid cube."

*Little ones hungry, yesssss? Here, something for you.* The front wall of grid changed shape, squeezing off to one side. Four gnarled balls floated into the cage, dropped a couple of objects, and the grid slammed shut again.

I never would have imagined I could be hungry in a situation like this. On the other hand, who had ever imagined a situation like this? My appetite, as perverse and unpredictable as ever, asserted itself with full force. We had been through a lot since lunch, which seemed like days ago, and all I'd eaten then was ketchup anyway.

"Wonder what this is?" I said, crawling toward one of the dropped objects, hoping it wasn't a slice of the head they had been discussing earlier.

"*I'm* not touching it. It's probably poison," Pete said.

"Why would they want to poison us? They think we're cute." I gingerly poked the object. It wasn't anything's head, at least—even 4-space creatures probably wouldn't give their luscious delicacies to pets. It was crumbly and bland-smelling, like bread or cake. Gigigi had been smart enough, seeing how we were built, to give us what must seem like her very thin slivers. But it was still too thick in the *ana* and *kata* direction to go inside my body, which had no *ana* and *kata* to it at all. I had to peel off a thin strip of it with my fingernail. I lifted it to my mouth.

*Yessss, little one. Go ahead, eat, eat. Little one needs some fattening up.*

But I paused, remembering the reversed ketchup. Was I reversed or not now? There was no way to tell. I had probably reversed back and forth dozens of times since leaving home. Being reversed wouldn't make any difference out here, logically. There might be other peculiarities to 4-space food, but if so, I might as well find out now. Anyway, I was starving. And what did I have to lose?

The stuff did not seem unwholesome. It tasted a little like gingerbread. The most surprising thing about eating it was Gigigi and Ramoom's reaction.

Shrieks of laughter, like symphonies of revving motorcycles.

*Ohhhhh! Did you see that? How darling, how sweet!*

*Sensational!*

*Do it again, again, little one. Eat more for us!*

"*Now* what's the matter with them?" Pete asked nervously.

"Who knows? But you might as well try some of this. Doesn't taste bad or make me feel weird." I peeled off another slice. "And eating something might improve your mood."

He looked doubtful but took my advice.

More peals of laughter like armies of lovesick bullfrogs.

*Charming, charming! How delicate and amusing.*

*Utterly delightful. So engrossingly sensual. Infinitely more entertaining than that stupid bat of yours.*

Watching Pete, I finally saw what it was they were exclaiming about. Since we were transparent, the chewing of the food, and the peristaltic action of the esophagus pushing it down into the stomach, were all clearly visible. It didn't seem all that charming and amusing to me.

Still, it was nice to know that they had a good-spirited side to their natures, that they were not complete ogres, that they had a sense of humor, however warped. It was even nice to know that we were not going to starve to death. And even though being lost in 4-space was the worst thing that had ever happened to me, I had to admit things could have been worse. We hadn't been eaten by a 4-space lion or crushed to death by a 4-space leaf fluttering down on us. We hadn't been rolled into tubes or folded into paper airplanes, as Omar had warned me so long ago.

But why had Omar kept telling me that anyone who got caught in 4-space had to be killed? If it was true, there had to be a reason for it. Somehow, I had the feeling that the reason was terribly obvious. But I didn't want to think about it now.

"Why do they keep laughing at us?" Pete said. "Why do they think we're so funny?"

"They like seeing the food going down inside us, that's all," I said. "You got any ideas about *why* we seem to be able to pick up their thoughts?"

"Mental telepathy? ESP?" he suggested as if that were the whole explanation.

"Sure, that's what it's called. But did it ever happen to you at home?"

"No."

"Well, I think I have an idea." I launched into the explanation I had come up with. So many things were different here. It wasn't only 4-space creatures' bodies that were *more* than ours. Their brains also had an added dimension that would certainly make their thought processes a lot more complicated and powerful than anything we were used to. It only made sense that four-dimensional brains, extending *ana* and *kata*, would have telepathic abilities.

"Yeah, but how come we understand their language?" Pete said. "I almost wish we didn't."

"I don't think we do understand their language. How could we? It's not actual words we're picking up. What we're getting must be just their basic thoughts, and also their emotions—4-space emotions so specific and highly developed that to 3-space creatures they seem like an actual language."

"Makes sense," Pete said, looking anxiously out of the cage. "But it doesn't make me like it any better here."

"But I wonder if there's any way we *could* communicate with them?" I said. "I bet our thoughts are too weak and thin for them to notice."

*Do you know, Gigigi, the most interesting thought has just occurred to me.*

*Yes, Ramoom? Look, aren't they sweet?*

*But doesn't it strike you as odd, Gigigi, that no one has ever before seen—not to mention even heard of—creatures such as this?*

"Do you think there *is* some way we could communicate with them?" Pete said, beginning to get excited. "Maybe we could get them to take us home. I've got to get out of here, Laura!"

"Do you think *I* like it here? Just try to calm down and listen to them. That's the only way we'll learn anything."

*And is it not also true that these could not possibly be the only two such creatures in existence? Nature does not work that way. There must be more of them somewhere, Gigigi. Many more.*

"Yes, there are!" Pete shouted at them. "We'll help you find them if you take us home!"

"Be quiet, Pete! I'm sure they can't understand English."

*Many more, Ramoom? Do you really think we could find them?*

And at that moment I knew the real reason Omar had been

so reluctant to take me into 4-space, so careful never to be seen by 4-space creatures. And I saw that a death penalty for being caught was not extreme at all. I remembered the analogy of a flat, two-dimensional world, completely unaware of the three-dimensional world on either side of it—and completely vulnerable to it. If such a world existed, people in 3-space would be able to reach in and pluck creatures off the surface whenever they wished. They would also be able to do anything else they wanted—crush buildings, reshape countrysides, control events in any way that might amuse them. And the 2-space people could do nothing to prevent it or to protect themselves. The creatures from the dimension above would have absolute power.

And our world would be in exactly the same situation—if these creatures ever found it.

*Perhaps we could, Gigigi. Whether or not they can actually think, we might be able to find out where they come from. The rest of their species might even be hiding somewhere not far from here. Do you not think that would be interesting? Imagine the possibilities. . . .*

For the first time I understood the inevitable and disastrous consequences of what I had done. Our situation was a lot worse than I had ever imagined. Somehow, 3-space had remained undiscovered all this time. But now, if we ever went back, we would be leading these 4-space creatures right to our world, laying bare and exposing our home to them.

"Did you hear that, Laura? They *want* to find out where we come from. They want to take us home! Maybe we can get them to do it right away!" Pete grabbed my arm, his heart quickening, his aorta swelling as blood rushed eagerly to his brain.

"No, Pete. No." I squirmed miserably away from him. Pete had it all wrong. We couldn't let them take us home. We couldn't go home at all unless we could figure out how to get there *without* showing them the way. Because if they discovered our home, then it wouldn't be home anymore, ever again.

# 13

*Come, my little ones. Outside, outside to watch morning. We eat, and watch morning come.*

There was a sharp tug, *kata* and above us. Then the cage was swinging again, back and forth, up and down, *ana* and *kata*.

On the other side of the grid, dark kaleidoscope patterns flashed by.

Pete, rubbing his eyes and groaning, had fallen asleep too. We both must have been so exhausted that even extreme nervous tension couldn't keep us awake.

"What do you mean, I got it all wrong?" Pete had demanded, last night, when I had pulled away from him. "Didn't you hear them? They want to help us find the way back."

"Oh, Pete, it's not that simple," I said, slumping against the grid.

"Yes, it is. Don't you understand?" His larynx was tense with excitement, making his voice shrill and high-pitched. "Maybe we *can* get out of this horrible place after all." He squeezed my hand, beaming at me. "Isn't it wonderful? This is the first good thing that's happened since we got here."

I looked away from him, not knowing what to say, my hand limp in his grasp. Maybe it would be better *not* to tell him the truth, he was so pitifully exuberant now. He was certainly easier to get along with when he was in a good mood. If he knew how hopeless our situation really was, he'd just get hostile again.

"What's the matter with you, Laura?" he said, his smile fading. "Look at me! You should be celebrating, not sulking."

"I'm sorry, Pete." I turned back to him, but I couldn't manage a smile. "I guess I just can't believe . . . it's going to be that easy to get home."

"There you go, being negative again!" he accused me, dropping my hand and scowling at me. "I'm so tired of your moodiness and depression. Being with you just makes everything worse. And I wish you'd wipe that mud off your face. I'm sick of looking at it."

I couldn't help remembering how differently Omar had reacted to my unhappiness the day Pete had walked off with Arlene. Omar had cared about me and tried to understand what was wrong; he had gone out of his way to make me feel better. All Pete could do was lash out and try to punish me. And here I was, trying to protect *his* feelings.

And so I lost control and lashed right back at him. "If you had a brain in your head, you'd know what was wrong!" I said. "We can't let them take us home. Don't you see? Our world is completely vulnerable to them. They could destroy everything. We can't go home unless we can get there *without* showing them the way. And how do you think we're going to do that, since we can't even get out of this cage? Got any ideas?"

"Oh, you're just being hysterical, inventing things to worry about," he said, with a gesture of disgust. The expression on his face was a lot more unattractive than the insides of his intestines. "What makes you think they'd *want* to destroy our world—even if they could?"

I noticed some throbbings of doting concern from Gigigi, who was still watching us—Ramoom had gone off to do something else. I tried to ignore her. "It's not that they would *plan* to destroy our world," I said, trying to sound reasonable and not hysterical. "It's just that they would have absolute power over it, because of being a dimension higher than us. They could do whatever they wanted to us, and no one could prevent it. That's why we can't do *anything* to let them find where we came from—even if it means we have to stay here for the rest of our lives." To protect 3-space, of course, was why it made sense that anybody who got caught in 4-space had to be killed. But I didn't mention that to Pete. Somehow—I wasn't sure exactly why—I didn't want him to know anything about Omar. Instead I added, sarcastically, "Still feel like celebrating, Pete?"

That was a mistake. He lunged at me and grabbed my shoulders, squeezing them painfully. "Listen, it's not *my* responsibility to stay here forever just because you have some crazy idea about what they'd do to our world. If I can get them to take me back, I will. And you can't do anything to stop me!"

"Just let go of me!" I said, wrenching away from him.

"If I want to go home, I will. And you can't stop me," he said again, sounding more self-righteous than angry now.

"What can I do to stop you? I can't even get out of this cage," I said, rubbing my shoulders. "Oh, come on, Pete. Let's not fight. It just makes everything worse."

"Don't blame me. You're the one who started it, by being in such a bad mood," he said, his voice petulant.

"Okay, okay, I'll try to be more positive." I sighed. "We're both tired. Maybe . . . things will look better in the morning."

He stared at me, then took a deep breath. "Yeah, maybe they will." Then he looked down, embarrassed. "Laura? I'm . . . sorry, if I hurt you," he said, a little sheepishly. "I didn't mean to. I just . . . was so excited about going home, and then . . ."

"It's okay, Pete," I said. "I can forgive you, this once."

And finally we curled up together on the floor of the cage. We both needed a little comfort. The next thing I knew it seemed to be early morning, and Gigigi was crooning at us, and carrying us outside. And everything was as hopeless as ever.

Air and fresher smells rushed into the cage. The grid swung open, two blobs dropped some hunks of food, two other blobs dropped something that glittered, the grid slammed shut.

*Eat, little ones. Eat . . . and see.* Gigigi's thoughts were like eager panting. *You eat, and try instrument Ramoom has made for you. You seeee rise of sun.*

"I dreamed . . . I was at home," Pete said, keeping his face away from me, as though he was trying not to cry.

I couldn't blame him. It was demoralizing to wake up and find ourselves the helpless prisoners of two monsters. "We should try to eat something," I said. "We'll probably need the strength."

Gigigi burbled with delight at the sight of our digestive processes. Then she was urging us again. *Try instrument. Ramoom made it for you. I know you will like. Try and you see.* The last crumb of gingerbread fell from my hand, and we rolled around on the pillowed floor as many cracked and grimy blobs shook the cage impatiently. *Try instrument! Gigigi want little ones try!*

| 101

"She must mean that thing she dropped in the cage." I crawled around the rocking cage until I found it. There was more light now. As the cage stabilized, I sat back on my heels and looked at the thing.

It had lenses and a wire frame, with two hooks that fit over the ears, like those special glasses jewelers wear or a funny pair of binoculars. A little stab of curiosity and excitement pierced through my miserable mood.

"What is it?" Pete said, crawling over to me.

"Some kind of glasses." I turned toward him. "Do you think it's really possible?"

"What's possible?"

"That these things can make it so that we can see 4-space the way 4-space creatures do? Not just cross sections, but solid four-dimensional objects. See? There's two lenses at one end and three at the other."

"I don't get it."

"It makes sense, Pete. Three-dimensional people need two eyes—binocular vision—in order to perceive depth, the third dimension. So in 4-space they need three eyes—trinocular vision—in order to *really* perceive *ana* and *kata*. This thing gives us three eyes, Pete." Fumbling with sudden eagerness, I slipped the hooks over my ears.

Beyond the grid I saw bleary smears of black and gray, and faint touches of lavender. A dark crouching shape billowed out of my view. *No look at Gigigi! Look at world. Look at rise of sun.*

Why was Gigigi so shy all of a sudden? Why didn't she want me to see her? But I was too busy to worry about that now. I concentrated on bringing the blurry world into focus, adjusting my eyes to the lenses. Triple images pulled together. Fuzzy surfaces grew sharp-edged. Space unfolded, expanded, and stretched away. It was like suddenly finding myself looking straight down from the top of the world's tallest skyscraper.

It was crazier than the cross sections. Everything was *more* than it should have been, many-faceted, infinitely complex. Each leaf had swollen into a miniature tree; each gray, emerging tree was an entire planet of foliage, seen from the inside and the outside at the same time. Nearby, the trunks all veered away from me as though I were lying on the ground looking up. But a little farther away they all seemed to stretch toward me as though growing on the inside of a deep crater, and beyond that they pointed down at me, as though I were looking at them from above. The sky, like the ground, kept showing up in unexpected places, underneath and behind the trees as well as *ana* and above them.

"Let me see now. My turn!" Pete said, made impatient by my exclamations of amazement.

"No, wait! Not yet!" I pulled away from him, focusing on the sky.

The lavender glow of morning was emerging not from one puny little direction, as in 3-space, but from every edge of the sky that I could see. The rising sun, about to appear, did not seem to be a point or a disk, but a vast ring that embraced the entire horizon. Blue and red spears of brightness shot out from all sides at once, continents of klieg lights going wild. Then the sky was too dazzling. "Here, take a look," I said, handing the glasses to Pete. I squeezed my eyes shut, dizzy and overwhelmed.

*Oh, a boring rise of sun, that is too bad. Tomorrow it will perhaps be nicer. Or the day after that. Or day after that. Or day after that. Little ones will see.*

That ruined it. I remembered where we were. And Gigigi didn't sound terribly eager to get rid of us.

*But did little one like?* That was Ramoom. *Can little ones understand how to use instrument?*

That was when I suddenly wondered *why* Ramoom had gone to the trouble to make the trinoculars for us. Was it simply to give us the experience of seeing things in full four-dimensional splendor out of the goodness of his heart? Or was it, maybe, to enable us to get around better—so we could lead them back the way we had come?

*I think so, Ramoom. See how it looks around?*

*But we must find out. We must find out exactly how much they understand. I have been working on a way to do that. Bring them back inside.*

*What kind of a way, Ramoom? Nothing that will hurt them. You must promise!*

*I have already made enough promises. Bring them inside.*

But just as the cage was lifted, I heard something in the distance. Was it a voice, singing? It was faint, but seemed to be approaching. And it was not just an emotion in my brain, but an actual sound, a rumbling, booming voice singing a vaguely familiar tune. "Tra la-la la!" echoed the voice across the rolling, tilting countryside. "Little brothers, here am I! Bringing luck and jollity!"

*Wait. Someone is coming.*

*But who could it be? No one ever comes this far out into the wilderness. Ramoom, what if someone . . . someone sees me?* I felt the horror in her mind at the thought of that.

*I don't like it.*

*He must not see me! And he must not find them.* Now Gigigi's emotions were shrill with panic. *They belong to us. No one else must see them.*

*For once I agree with you, Gigigi. No one else must find them —yet. Not until we know more. Not until we are in control.*

*I do not understand you, Ramoom. But why do you hesitate? Bring them inside.*

*Not safe enough. He might be searching and snooping. Somewhere else. . . . I have it! The pit. Now go hide your ugly face from the stranger.*

The cage lurched wildly.

"What's happening?" The trinocular glasses tumbled from Pete's eyes. "Now what are they doing with us?"

"I don't know. Shut up and listen."

*But not the pit, Ramoom! That is truly unsafe. You know what we sometimes find in there. Please!*

*They are secure enough inside the cage. I know; I made it. The pit is the only place where they will be safe from prying eyes. Go into the house and hide yourself, or you will be seen.*

*Not the pit, Ramoom! Please, no!*

*Enough! I will do what I wish . . . or I will desert you, Gigigi.*

And then the cage was being lowered into what seemed to be a smelly hole full of leaves and dirt. There was a heavy thud above us and the hole went dark—just as I got my hands on the trinoculars.

"Ugh! This place stinks."

"But Pete, did you hear anything? Like maybe a voice? The creature they're hiding us from?"

"I'm not sure. I was too busy trying to see through those glasses. I don't like it down here."

"I could almost swear it was a voice. . . . A voice I've heard before." But where had I heard it? Too much was happening all at once for me to be able to think clearly. All I was really sure of was that the voice was associated with something unpleasant. It was like a reminder of a nightmare I had worked very hard at trying to forget. I did have the feeling, though, that it had something to do with Omar, and with some kind of secret I wasn't supposed to know about.

"How could you hear it before, Laura?"

"Shhhh. See if you can hear it too."

Nothing at first. Then the song again, muffled, but growing louder. "You hear it, Pete?"

"Barely. Doesn't sound familiar to *me*," he said.

I also sensed vibrations in the earth. Not the rhythm of two feet tramping closer, more complicated than that. Was there more than one of them? What would happen if they *did* find us and take us away from Gigigi and Ramoom? Would our situation be better or worse?

Maybe it was some creature coming to carry out the law—to kill us before we gave anything away.

But before I had a chance to worry about that, I became aware of a gnawing, chomping sound very close to us. A sandy slithering, a shifting of soil, the rustle of pebbles dislodged. A little light had penetrated around the object covering the hole, and my eyes were adjusting. I slipped on the trinoculars and peered out through the grid of the cage.

I screamed. Six slitted eyes were staring at us above two spherical mouths ringed with fangs.

"Laura! What . . ." Then Pete screamed too.

However horrible it looked to him, it probably looked worse to me. With the trinoculars on, I could see that the two heads were attached to a single body of braided cylinders. And I could not look away from the eyes—I was riveted in the same way that a trapped bird is hypnotized by a snake. That's what this was. Some kind of burrowing 4-space snake with two heads.

The heads lunged. Two sets of fangs sank into the grid. A tail thrashed above, knocking more pebbles and dirt onto the roof of the cage. Sand sprinkled on my head and feet. The grid rattled, the entire cage trembled as the snake violently shook it.

Whimpering, we crouched together against the back wall, as far from the snake as we could get. But what if the grid sprang open? What if the cage was not as secure as Ramoom thought?

One head chewed at the grid. The other darted to the side, poking, probing, twisting at the bars. Were 4-space snakes intelligent enough to open latches? And if they were, which head would get to us first? Would they fight over us? Or would they share us, one for each?

We were both screaming again. The snake kept biting and wriggling.

There was a click. The grid shuddered and began to open.

"Laura, it didn't get in, did it? *Did it?*"

"Yes, yes, it's getting in," I sobbed.

One of the heads was trying to work its way through the gap where the grid had opened. The hole we were in seemed to be too narrow to allow the cage to open completely. But now the two heads were working together, one of them pushing earth and stones aside to allow the cage to open wider, the other continuing to wedge itself toward us. Soil shifted. The grid shivered. The gap widened. The head inched closer.

Sudden light splashed into the hole. The cage sailed up out of the ground, tilting from the weight of the snake that still clung to it with one head. The grid swung wide. We tumbled toward the other set of fangs, opened for us.

Two four-fingered hands closed around the snake's heads, pulled them away and flung it to the ground. At the same time a six-fingered hand slammed the grid, which felt like bedsprings as my body hit it and was bounced back into the cage. I heard Gigigi's voice shouting what sounded like curses, and her thoughts: *Ohhhh, my little ones, my pooor, pooor little ones. Gigigi save. Gigigi not let bad thing hurt you.* And a moment later we were back inside the house, the cage hanging from its hook, as Gigigi, still keeping carefully out of sight, continued to soothe us.

I remembered that, when Gigigi had first given us the trinoculars, she hadn't wanted us to see what she really looked like. That meant she assumed that we understood their use. But I didn't want them to know how much we understood. I was still wearing them—that was why I had seen her hands as hands, not blobs. Now I quickly pushed them to the top of my head, like a tiara—as though that was what I thought they should be used for.

They argued for a while, Gigigi accusing, Ramoom defending himself. Their dialogue shifted, Ramoom insisting that he must do the "experiment" on us, soon, so that they could learn as much about us as possible before anyone else came along. There didn't seem to be anything Gigigi could do to prevent it.

"I don't like the sound of this experiment," Pete said weakly.

"Neither do I." We had both barely recovered from the snake's attack, and already Ramoom was setting up equipment *kata* and below the cage.

**14**

I tried to cheat at first, playing dumb—until Ramoom figured out how to motivate me.

I couldn't help being impressed when I got my first good look at the maze. Ramoom's 4-space brain had to be pretty formidable for him to have designed and constructed something this complicated so quickly.

It was built inside a hypercube. It seemed to be about thirty feet on a side, riddled with snarled corridors and ramps, blind corners and dead ends. It was far worse than the hedge mazes I had encountered at home, which were easy enough to get lost in despite the fact that they were essentially only two-dimensional problems.

This one went in three directions, mazes piled on top of mazes, devilishly confusing.

Especially since, being inside a hypercube, the walls stood up in the *ana* and *kata* direction. Which meant that, even out here in 4-space, a person inside it could not see over them.

Ramoom plucked Pete out of the cage. While he was moving him, I took a hasty look at the structure through the trinoculars—without them, I could see nothing but fragmented cross sections of it. He pushed Pete inside one of the two openings in the maze, then closed it off. Now there was only one way out. I quickly pushed the trinoculars back on top of my head again before Ramoom looked back at me.

*This is a game*, Ramoom thought at us. *The one on the outside must tell the one on the inside how to get out of the box. If you do it very quickly, I will give you some nice food. Start now.*

"Hurry, Laura!" Pete shouted *ana* at me. "Which way?" It was easy to hear him, since some boundary cubes were missing from the hypercube; the maze was the 4-space equivalent of an open box.

It was a clever test. Since the walls inside the open-topped maze went in the *ana* and *kata* direction, and since the cage I was in hung "above" the maze in the *ana* direction, with the trinoculars on I could look "down" into it and see the way out quite clearly. I was like one of those people sitting on an elevated chair in the middle of a hedge maze, who can see the whole thing and give directions to the seriously lost. Only with instructions from me would Pete be able to get out without wandering around for hours and hours.

And then Ramoom would know that we could understand his instructions. He would know we were intelligent and had our own language. And he would know that we could give complicated directions about how to get from one place to another. If Ramoom knew those things about us, he would also know that he could force us to help him find where we had come from.

But Ramoom wasn't going to know any of that if I could help it.

"I can't, Pete!" I called down to him, the trinocs perched on top of my head. "I'm afraid you're going to be in there for a while."

"What's the matter with you?" he screamed, and swore at me. Then I heard his delicate little footsteps as he started down a corridor.

Of course, my natural impulse was to watch Pete and tell him how to get out of the maze. But I fought against it. I had to act stupid and ruin Ramoom's experiment. That would prove to him that we had no language, no intelligence, and could not help him find where we had come from. And then he might leave us alone and eventually forget about us. After that, if we were lucky, we might be able to sneak away without being followed. It was our only chance of getting home without endangering our universe.

And maybe I could really carry it off. I began to let myself hope.

*It is not working, Ramoom.* Gigigi seemed to feel as pleased about that as I was.

*The one* ana *is doing nothing . . . maddening, perverse creatures!*

*Do not blame them, Ramoom, if they are not what you want them to be. And do not get angry at them, or I will—*

*Or you will what, twisted one? You cannot stop me. Here, little obstinate thing, you wear them like this!* He reached in and none too gently adjusted the trinocs over my eyes. Then he plunked me down on the edge of the open cage, my feet dangling into empty space, and pointed my head *ana* down at the maze. He repeated his instructions.

I saw now that the maze was not simple and unadorned like

a purely businesslike rat maze at home. It was intricately carved, with curving, curlicued lintels over the doorways, and turrets and pointed archways, and balconies with railings that had faces sculpted in them. It was as elaborately detailed as a mosque, like something out of a Russian fairy tale. It didn't make sense that Ramoom would go to so much unnecessary trouble just to make it look pretty. But maybe he hadn't. Maybe that was just the way artifacts *were* in 4-space, automatically, because of the extra dimension.

Meanwhile, there was Pete, a flat transparent thing blundering around inside it, shrinking to a pink line every time he turned to the side. He stopped in a little room with two exits. "Help me, Laura! Which way do I go here?" Pete screamed, and kicked the wall.

I pressed my lips together, fighting the urge to call out to him.

"Please, Laura!" Pete wailed. "There's something terrible about this place, an evil feeling. *Please!*"

Maybe if I helped Pete just this once, Ramoom wouldn't notice. I glanced up to check on him.

And got my first good look at a 4-space person through the trinocs.

I almost screamed, it was so unexpected. Even with all my experience, I could barely make sense out of Ramoom. It was his head that was the problem, a hypersphere, a bulbous shape that curved out and around upon itself in the *ana* and *kata* direction. Think of a deformed elephant head with two fat trunks, both wrapped around it. Think of an octopus tied in knots. Blend them both together. Throw in some pulpy features. The result would be a mild and benign approximation of Ramoom's face.

The eyes watched the maze, the third between and *ana* the other two. Below and *kata* the eyes sprouted the piglike, threenostrilled nose. The double cylindrical mouth stretched around the face in a fixed, manic grimace.

"*Please,* Laura! Which way?" Pete cried pathetically.

I sensed Ramoom's mirth. His monstrous mouth twisted around into a grin; creases and folds like thick cables sprang out in three directions from his lips and eyes. His face was a terrain of troughs and chasms deep enough for me to fall into.

I tore my eyes away. I saw how precariously I was hanging *ana* above the maze and struggled against dizziness. Pete was turning back and forth in front of the two doorways, changing with each movement from a line to a pink flake. "Don't take the ramp!" I screamed at him, and pushed the trinocs up on top of my head.

I heard Pete's feet tapping along the zigzag corridor. A moment later he reached the next intersection. "Which way now?"

He deserved an explanation. "I can't tell you, Pete. Then he'll know we have language. He'll know we can give directions. Then he'll make us help him find 3-space."

"Let him!" he howled. "Let him help us find 3-space. And *get me out of here!*"

I gritted my teeth.

*Little ones do not understand, Ramoom. You make them unhappy, pointlessly. Face the truth, stubborn one. Your precious experiment is a failure.*

*Shut up! It is the one* ana *that pretends it does not understand. It must be as perverse and infuriating a creature as you, Gigigi. It needs a tiny touch of persuasion, that is all. . . .*

*What are you doing, Ramoom? Where are you going?* The indistinct bulk of Gigigi ballooned and then shrank away after him.

I quickly slipped on the trinocs and peered down *kata.* I found the exit from the maze and then followed the tilting, crenellated corridors back from it toward Pete, searching for a quick path. It wasn't easy without a pencil to mark the way. But Pete sounded in pretty bad shape. And it wouldn't prove anything to Ramoom if he thought Pete had found the way out on his own without instructions from me. What I didn't want him to know was that we had language.

It also occurred to me that it might be to my own advantage to learn the best escape route from the maze. I wondered what Ramoom meant by "persuasion."

"Okay, Pete, I found it." But I looked up for an instant first. The room seemed crazily distorted through the trinocs, full of impossible shapes. But I had enough practice now to be certain that Gigigi and Ramoom were both somewhere else for the moment. "Remember this, Pete, because I'm telling it fast. Take the middle door. Then at the next intersection go left, down the ramp. Then you'll come to three doorways. Take the *ana* one. . . ."

I concentrated, calling out directions to Pete, trying to fix the path in my own mind. ". . . then take the way that makes a U-turn. When you get to the fork, take the *kata* ramp—"

I was interrupted by the sounds of a struggle and then a heavy thud. *Ramoom, no! Let me in! Unlock this door! You cannot do that thing. Let me in. Please let me in!*

What was Ramoom going to do now, without Gigigi to protect us? I pushed the trinocs up on my head and stared placidly off into the distance, doing my best to look stupid.

Ramoom loomed up in front of me, floating eyes, the bulb of his nose, veiny cross sections bulging and fusing. *Here is something new for you to admire, clever one.* He pushed the trinocs roughly down over my eyes again.

Ramoom held it gingerly by its tail, a hairy thrashing thing the size of a large dog. It had three little red eyes, and lots of curving tusks, and eight short legs, kicking wildly. It emitted a piercing, enraged squeal. It made me think of a wild pig—

except that pigs only have hooves, and this thing had two front legs equipped with claws. It arched its back, caught one of Ramoom's fingers with a talon, and struck savagely with its head, sinking teeth into flesh.

*Aaieee! Impatient beast!* Ramoom swatted it with one of his other hands and then clamped two fingers around its neck to keep it in place. *But I can hardly blame it. Do you see how pitifully skinny it is?* Ramoom's tone was mocking. *The poor little thing is near starvation, I fear. That makes it think quickly when there is fresh meat to be found. You will be amazed at the speed of those little legs!*

He swung it away from me and dropped it into the middle of the maze. It snorted thickly, its snout scraping the floor. Then it took off fast, heading in a direct route for Pete.

And Pete, still following my directions, was running to meet it.

"No, Pete! He put a pig thing in there. Turn around!" I shrieked, trying to find another path. "Go back! Take . . . the first door on the left."

Then Ramoom lifted Pete out of the cage and set him down next to me.

"Oh, thank God," I said. "He was only—"

Ramoom pulled the trinocs from my eyes and thrust them at Pete. *Now, we mustn't have the stupid little one on top, must we? Oh, noooo. Too dangerous.* And then I was swung through the air. Walls sprang up *ana* around me. Ramoom's hand vanished. *Not to mention, it is only fair to share the experience.*

I spun around, frantically scanning the 4-space view inside the maze. I couldn't see over the walls, but I could put the interior cross sections together. I was in a small triangular room with three carved doorways. I remembered this room, from looking *kata* down at the maze. I knew the way out from here, without help from Pete, as long as I could avoid—

*Oh, dear me! Almost forgot to reset the lever.* Ramoom chuckled merrily.

The maze shuddered around me. Hinges squealed, sprockets shifted. And with a great wooden clacketing, walls sprang apart and slammed together; partitions rotated and fell through slots; the floor opened like a trapdoor beneath me and dropped me, sprawling, into a shadowy chamber.

Ramoom's contraption was even more impressive than I had realized. With the flick of a lever, he could switch all the walls around. I was now in the middle of a totally new and unfamiliar maze.

Behind me, I heard the clatter of racing hooves, and a moist whinny of anticipation.

# 15

"Which way, Pete? Hurry!" I yelled. I bounded away from the animal sounds, through a diamond-shaped doorway, onto a dim ramp that corkscrewed steeply around a fat column carved like a totem pole.

What if the ramp was a dead end and the thing cornered me up there? "Hurry, Pete! Should I take this ramp?"

"I . . . don't know." He sounded panicky. "It's hard for me to see. These glasses . . . and that place is so confusing."

I groaned and cursed him. But I couldn't wait. The pig thing was already snuffling in the chamber I had just left. I started up the ramp, praying it was not a dead end. It was slow going because the ramp was so dimly lit and steeply sloped. I tried to pull myself up by the carvings that jutted out from the central column. They weren't much help, because I could only see them in cross section without the trinocs. As soon as I got a good grip on one noselike extrusion and tried to push past, it would change shape and shrink away, leaving me grasping at air. And then a wooden arm would spring out unexpectedly below my knees, tripping me, and I would slip backwards again.

The ramp grew steeper as it ascended. At least the pig thing, behind me on the ramp now, was having problems too, its hooves squeaking and scrabbling on the slippery floorboards. But it still seemed to be gaining on me. It had three eyes and wouldn't be confused by cross sections. I began to hear the splintery tearing sound of talons ripping into wood. It was pulling itself up by its claws. Claws that could penetrate wood so easily would sink through my 3-space flesh as if it were soft butter.

"No, Laura. Wrong way. It's a dead end!" Pete called out.

I had no breath left to scream at him. I considered turning around and trying to slip past the creature. But with my limited vision, I'd probably just end up impaling myself on a tusk. I kept going.

The good news, I tried to tell myself, was that with Pete up there guiding me, Ramoom wouldn't get the idea we were an intelligent species. Though it would have been nicer if we could have convinced him of that without me getting gored and devoured.

The ramp leveled off. I ran forward, praying that Pete had been wrong, and there would be a way out. But there was only a blank, curving wall.

I could hear Pete screaming at Ramoom to save me. But from Ramoom I sensed only bitter disappointment at our failure, and no desire to help me at all.

I cowered against the wall. It was dark in here, but there was just enough light to see the cross sections appear over the edge of the slope: the four sharp points of the tusks sprouting into uplifted cones, the furry snuffling blob of the snout, the three floating red eyes.

And then the eyes ballooned toward me as the hooves drummed across the floor. The thing grunted and leapt, and the hot stink of its breath was on my face.

"No! We can't let it happen like this!" said a familiar lisping voice, seeming to come from within my ear.

I felt something inside my nose, pulling me in a direction that was, even out here in 4-space, completely unexpected. And everything rushed around more wildly than it ever had before.

# 16

I leaned against a curving wall. Ahead of me stretched a long and brightly lit corridor.

Something crashed against the wall at my back with enough force to push me staggering away from it. I turned and saw a cross section of tusk break through. From the other side of the wall came furious squeals of disappointment.

That had been Omar's voice inside my ear, there was no doubt about it. And then something had pulled me over the wall—over the *ana* and *kata* wall that could not be crossed in 4-space.

"Omar?" I whispered. "Omar, where are you?"

Faintly, inside my head, I heard a voice singing. "Tra la-la la! Tra la-la la! Don't expect from me a lie. If you're captured, you must die!"

And that was when I remembered where I had heard the same voice before—the voice of the creature that Ramoom had hidden us from only an hour ago. It was back in 3-space, the first time I had been reversed, when I had gone over to Omar's house and begged him to flip me over. I had inadvertently looked inside his house, against his wishes, and heard the music. *And I had seen a 4-space creature in Omar's kitchen.*

I had talked myself out of believing it at the time, unable to face the gruesome fact of that living blob inside Omar's house. But now I was more experienced, not so sensitive or easily shocked. And I knew I had seen and heard that creature another time too, on my very first trip into 4-space. It had been singing the same tune with different words: "Tra la-la la! Tra la-la la! Little brothers, here am I! Bringing luck and jollity!"

"Laura, how did you do that? How did you get across that wall?"

But what had that 4-space creature been doing in Omar's kitchen? They weren't supposed to know about us. And what had it been doing only an hour ago, so close to us in 4-space? I couldn't figure it out. What was going on here?

Pete was shouting at me. "You better hurry! It's going to break through the wall."

I spun around. There was a bulge in the flimsy wall, and the wood was beginning to split as the pig thing battered its head against it. I took off down the corridor.

*Amazing! Fantastic! I can hardly believe it.* Ramoom's anger had vanished. *The creature went through the wall. How is that possible?*

I reached an intersection, two corridors branching off to the left and right with a balcony between them. I stepped out onto the balcony and looked up and *ana*. I saw Ramoom's purple eye far above and, across from it, a distorted solid rectangle of cage, with a cross-sectional slice of Pete's gut at one edge of it. "Get me out of here, Pete!" I yelled. "I don't want that thing near me again. You find the way yet?"

"I think so." He didn't sound so sure. "Take the left . . . I mean, take the *right* fork."

I heard the hooves again. I didn't wait. I only hoped Pete knew what he was doing.

Down another ramp. A left turn along a columned gallery to another intersection with a nice safe corridor in one direction. In the other direction a narrow bridge, woven out of ropelike fibers, dangled off into space. It appeared to end abruptly in midair.

"Take the bridge," Pete called.

"But it doesn't go anywhere!"

"*I'm* giving the directions! It's the fastest way out. And the pig thing probably won't want to get on it."

That made sense. And the reason the bridge looked to me as though it ended in empty space must be that it stretched out into a cross section of 4-space I couldn't see from here. Holding my breath, I stepped onto it.

It was like trying to walk across a long narrow hammock. I pulled the elastic mesh as high as I could around me as it bucked and swayed in all the usual directions, plus *ana* and *kata*. It didn't help that it seemed to end in the middle of its span, so I had no idea how long it was. As I crept forward, it extended itself ahead of me.

"How long is this thing, Pete?"

"Just keep going. You've hardly even started."

"Great," I muttered. My sweaty hands kept slipping on the fibers as I tilted back and forth. Every fast movement I made created 4-space waves that rippled away and came billowing back, rolling my feet up higher to the sides. It was going to take forever, even if I didn't get bounced off before I reached the end.

I sensed new tremors behind me. Was the pig thing getting on the bridge? I tried to move faster, not daring to turn and look back.

Then I heard gnawing. The rope beneath my right foot quivered, and a moment later suddenly sprang away. I tripped, creating more turbulence as I dragged myself upright again. I inched more slowly along the dancing bridge, getting seasick. No, the pig thing wasn't following me. It was smarter than that. Like the snake, it had a four-dimensional brain. It knew that when it ate through the bridge I would fall, and probably be hurt badly enough so that I couldn't run. And then it would have no trouble getting to me.

The cord I was squeezing with my left hand suddenly went limp and dropped away. Only by falling flat on my stomach and clinging with all my fingers did I keep from tumbling off. And in that position I continued to crawl forward. I didn't know what else to do.

The bridge tossed and churned. Another rope fell away, then another. It wouldn't be long now before I'd be hanging from a single strand. I knew my arms would give way soon after that. My strength was almost gone already.

"How much farther, Pete?"

"Don't worry about that! Just keep going!" But I could tell from his voice that he had little hope. There wasn't much left of the bridge.

I was trying to balance my outstretched body on two ropes now, my elbows and ankles wrapped around them. The one on the right began to tremble. I let go of it and quickly grabbed the other one with both hands and feet. The right-hand rope dropped away. Now I was hanging upside down, staring up *and* out of the maze.

Up into Ramoom's three yellow-veined eyes and a section of chapped, flaky lip. A thick slab of tongue protruded, deeply fissured like the bottom of a mudhole. I became aware again of a distant thudding, and Gigigi's anguished thoughts. The rope fluttered. My hands loosened as I felt it begin to give way.

Then I was carried into the air and tossed into the cage.

I lay there panting, dimly aware of their thoughts washing over me, of Gigigi returning and Ramoom trying to calm her down.

"I'm sorry, Laura," Pete said as though he meant it, his hand stroking my back. "I tried to get you out of there sooner. I really did."

"I know, Pete. It's okay. It was worth it . . . if it makes him think we can't show him the way to 3-space."

"Huh?" Pete said, his hand stopping abruptly. "But, Laura, I *am* going to help him find the way home, if I can."

"Don't say that, Pete!" I sat up and faced him. "You know what will happen if he finds 3-space. You *can't!*"

"Sorry, Laura," Pete said firmly, shaking his head. His curly hair stood up in grimy, matted tufts around his face, his features drawn and damp with sweat. "I'm not staying here if there's any way to get home. I just wish I had a better feeling about which way it was."

It was a good thing Pete didn't have a better sense of direction. Still, Ramoom would probably be able to find the way. That must be their lantern out there where we had left the rope. Ramoom could find that easily enough. Once he followed the rope back to where we started, it wouldn't take him very long to check out the whole circumference of the area. 3-space had to be in there somewhere. But what I said to Pete was "Well, if *you* don't know which way it is, there's no way *he* can find it."

"I'm going to try, Laura."

At the moment, Ramoom was telling something important to Gigigi, something that amazed and frightened her enough to make her forget how angry she was at him.

"Yeah, what about that?" whispered Pete. "How did you do it, Laura? How did you get through that wall?"

"Huh?" Then I remembered. Back in the maze, Omar's voice inside my ear. And then being pulled, in some impossible direction, over the *ana* and *kata* wall. As though it were a mere 3-space wall back at home.

But what did it mean? That Omar was out here, hiding somewhere, waiting for the chance to rescue us—or to kill us? And what about the singing 4-space creature who sounded exactly like the one who had visited Omar that night? Were he and Omar together?

"Pete, can I have the trinocs?"

"Sure." He handed them to me. "But how did you get over that wall? I thought you said you couldn't do that out here."

"Wait a minute." I didn't understand what had happened inside the maze, but Omar's voice—and his ability to take me over the wall—might be hopeful signs. Maybe there *was* a way we could escape without leading Ramoom to 3-space. But now I didn't trust Pete enough to tell him about it. The more he knew, the more he could spill to Ramoom. I slipped on the trinocs and looked out of the cage.

*Yessssss, my little ones. No one will hurt you again. Now Ramoom knows how special you are, as I always knew. Now he understands. And Gigigi will always protect you.*

I was startled by the sudden sight of her face through the trinocs. She looked very much like Ramoom. She had more hair, a vertical black fan framing her face, patterned with four jagged streaks of white, like lightning bolts. That was the only indication of the difference in gender between them. Her face was equally craggy, jutting and creased—equally hideous to me.

And yet there *was* something else different about her face. Something wrong with it. All at once, their frequent references to some deformity of hers—and her fear of being seen—came flooding back to me: *A blemish such as you . . . My poor face has nothing to do with overindulgence. . . . Your own, shall we say, peculiarities . . . No look at Gigigi . . . Twisted one . . .*

I stared, concentrating, looking back and forth between her and Ramoom.

And then I had it. His third eye was *ana* the other two; Gigigi's was *kata.* His nose was *kata* from the eyes; Gigigi's was *ana.* To someone more familiar with *ana* and *kata* than I was, and with 4-space anatomy, these discrepancies would be immediately striking, probably monstrous. The two of them were opposites—wherever Ramoom's face went one way, Gigigi's went the other. But I had to study her face for a long moment and think hard about what the differences meant before I realized the obvious.

Gigigi was reversed.

# 17

*Feed them, Gigigi. Hurry. We must keep them happy. If they can go through walls, that means . . .*

*Means what, Ramoom?*

*Never mind. Feed them. We will be going soon.*

"Don't just sit there staring, Laura. Answer me! How did you get over that wall?"

"Uh . . . the same way I did it on the roof. Remember?"

"You said that didn't work out here. You're hiding something."

*Going where, Ramoom?*

*Back to where they came from. Back to their own kind. Unless they do not want us to take them home, that is.*

"Hey!" Pete called out. "Don't get the wrong—"

"Shut up, Pete!"

"Shut up yourself! I want to go home. I don't believe anything will happen if Ramoom helps us find 3-space. That's just some hysterical idea of yours."

Gigigi dropped food into the cage. I gobbled it down, hungry after all the running around I had done in the maze. And I didn't feel like arguing with Pete. The less I said to him, the better.

Gigigi and Ramoom had not yet become jaded; they were still vastly amused by the spectacle of three-dimensional digestion. *And do you not think, Gigigi, that others might be amused by such a sight as this? They might be willing to do much for us to obtain the privilege of watching.*

*Ramoom, you promised! These creatures belong to me. They are our secret!*

*These two creatures, yes, ungenerous one! You may keep these two as your own personal, secret playthings eternally for all I care. But what about others, where they came from? I would not be breaking any promise if I found others, for purposes of display. Or, I should say, to share with the world. It does not seem fair to keep this wonder all to ourselves. . . .*

"Well, there goes 3-space," I couldn't help muttering.

"But . . ." Pete said. I could tell by the expression on his face that he was finally beginning to understand what would happen if Ramoom found 3-space. But he still wouldn't admit that I had been right all along. "Maybe, uh, we could make some kind of a bargain with him," he said weakly. "Like, if he brought us home, maybe he could take somebody else—like Mrs. Bowers, maybe—and then, leave our world alone after that."

"Oh, sure," I said. "I sure would trust Ramoom to make a bargain and then stick to it, when he has total power and we don't have any. Great idea, Pete. That solves everything."

"I don't see *you* coming up with a better plan!"

"Maybe I will if you give me a chance!"

I tried to ignore Gigigi and Ramoom and figure a few things out. I was pretty sure Omar could see us and was aware of what was going on—he had saved me at precisely the right moment. And it was just like Omar. He had done exactly the same things back at home, hiding invisibly in 4-space and watching. The problem was, now *we* were in 4-space. So where was Omar watching us *from*?

And that wasn't the only problem. *Why* was Omar—possibly in cahoots with the opera-singing 4-space creature—hiding and watching us? If they could save me from the pig thing, that meant they also had the ability to get me and Pete out of the cage and away from Ramoom and Gigigi. So why weren't they doing that? The longer they delayed, the more likely we would be to give in to coercion and spill the information about 3-space. If they were planning to rescue us, what were they waiting for?

I thought of the new words to the song, and Omar's frequent warnings. And I could only conclude that they *weren't* planning to rescue us. Maybe all they could do was observe us to make sure we were not doing anything to endanger 3-space—and then stop us before we did.

I forced myself to be realistic about it, unpleasant as it was. And realistically, I knew that two individual lives were utterly dispensable when balanced against the safety of the entire 3-space universe. And as long as we were out here, the universe wouldn't be secure. Omar didn't *want* them to kill us; he was probably making them wait until the last possible moment. But when that moment came, they wouldn't have any choice.

Then why had Omar bothered to save me from the pig thing? Because he would rather have me die painlessly. The more I thought about it, the more grim sense it made. I couldn't even blame Omar. What else could he do to correct the terrible mistake he had made? As soon as Pete made another slip, they would have to act. All I could do was try to keep Pete's mouth closed for as long as possible. But it was still only a matter of time. We had to die: It was the inevitable result of our coming out here and getting caught. Omar had told me many times.

Unless . . .

Unless I could do something that would throw Ramoom and Gigigi off completely; something that would absolutely convince them that 3-space did not exist and that there was no way they would ever find any other creatures like us.

*You see now, my warped companion, that my little test was a success. They understand. They can communicate. They know directions. And now that they have eaten, it is time for our trip.*

Gigigi's feelings were hurt. Ramoom teased her often about her deformity, but she remained sensitive about it. *Now you are imagining things, Ramoom. They are sweet little creatures, and quick. But that does not mean they have true intelligence or understanding. And it is not necessary to insult me! The terrible accident that changed me was not my fault.*

What accident? How had Gigigi been reversed? I got reversed by going up into 4-space and turning around. Where would Gigigi go to have that happen to her?

*You will see how much they understand. But there is no time to quibble. We must hurry, before . . .*

"Good," Pete said. "I'm ready to get out of here. There's nothing *we* can do to stop him from—"

"Shhh! I'm trying to listen!"

*Before what, Ramoom? What are you afraid of? You are always worrying. Be relaxed, like Gigigi. We can take our time. They are safe with us.*

*Your brain is as addled as your face! They may not be as safe as you think. And do not try to interfere. I warn you, I can leave you at any time. And you know that no one else would have the stomach to be a companion of one such as you.*

130

*They may not be as safe as you think.* That was it. Ramoom had seen me being pulled through the wall of the maze. To him, we were evanescent, easily vanishing. If we could go through walls of mazes, we could get out of cages too—if we were clever enough to think of it. He didn't know I hadn't done it on my own and that we really were safe in the cage. He wanted us to show him where 3-space was before we got smart and got away.

Gigigi's reversal had given me another idea—an idea that might be the answer to *where* Omar was watching us from. Now I had the beginnings of a plan. It was riskier than I would have liked. But I had no time to come up with anything else.

"I just can't stand it here anymore," Pete was whining. "And you can't stop me if I want to help him find the way back! Anyway, you're nuts to think one creature like Ramoom could destroy the whole universe. You worry too much, that's all."

Gigigi had said that to Ramoom. Pete was saying it to me. And I had said it to Omar. Naturally he had been worried about taking me into 4-space. It really had been a colossally stupid thing for him to do, though I was as much to blame as he was. But maybe I could still do something to make up for it. I hoped Omar would catch on in time.

*Now you must listen carefully to your friend Ramoom.* Ramoom stared into the cage. He was not a pretty sight, his four hands twisting together like a ball of writhing reptiles, the bewildering manifolds of his face split apart by a smile that seemed to stretch all the way around his head. The inside of his mouth was like an aerial view of a bombed-out city. *You must do as I say, so that I can take you home. You must trust your friend Ramoom, yesssss. . . .*

I had to think fast to work out the details of my plan. I knew now why Ramoom had not bothered to shut the door of the cage after the maze experiment. He knew we were earthbound creatures, ruled by gravity. The cage was high enough so that a fall from it would be crippling, if not fatal. On our scale, it was a good forty or fifty feet above the floor. So why close it? They could probably see us better with the door opened anyway.

*Now, can you demonstrate to Ramoom the sound for the affirmative? Say it loudly.*

I glared at Pete, my lips pressed together, trying to will him not to obey. Pete pouted back at me, thrusting out his lower lip.

*Tell Ramoom, or he cannot take you home!*

"Keep your mouth shut, Pete!" I ordered him.

Pete stared up at Ramoom (easy for him, because without the trinocs he couldn't see what he really looked like), cupped his hands over his mouth and yelled, "Yes! Yes, yes, yes!"

"Byeththth?" Ramoom boomed out, using his 4-space vocal cords for the first time since we had arrived. "Byeththth?"

"Yes!" Pete screamed back, nodding frantically. "Yes!"

*Very good, very smart, little one. And the negative?*

"No! No, no, no!"

"Gnoooo! Gnoooo!" Ramoom echoed. *Very, very helpful. Now you can easily point Ramoom in the right direction.*

"See, you can't stop me—" Pete started to say. "Hey! Where'd you go?"

Without the trinocs, Pete could only see one cross section of 4-space at a time, and I had left his line of sight. I stopped climbing for a moment, clinging to the outside of the cage, and turned to Ramoom and shouted, "Yes, yes, yes!" pointing above me. I began climbing again, praying that Omar would not kill me before he figured out what I was trying to do.

Pete, who had managed to learn how to scan 4-space by turning his head back and forth, finally saw where I was. "Laura! Are you out of your mind? Come back! You're going to kill yourself!"

"If somebody else doesn't do it first!" I shouted. Again, I turned toward Ramoom and pointed up *ana*. "Yes, yes, yes!" I told him, and went on climbing.

It wasn't easy, climbing up around the outside of a hypercube. It didn't just have six sides, like an ordinary cube. It had twenty-four. They were connected at sixteen corners, and jutted out at peculiar angles, so some of the time I was crawling nearly upside down. Each time I reached one of the edges— there were thirty-two of *them*—I wouldn't know what direction to expect next. My best guide was gravity. If I just kept going whichever way felt closest to up and *ana*, I'd eventually end up on top of the cage—if one thing or another didn't stop me first.

*Oh, Ramoom. You have frightened the poor thing out of its wits. I must put it back inside before it falls.*

I was lucky that the little cubes that made up the surface of the grid were just the right size for my hands and feet to fit easily inside them. And the cage was solid enough so that my weight didn't make it swing. But it was more frightening than the bridge, because it was so much higher. I did not look down, but kept my eyes focused on the cubes just above my hands.

*Wait, Gigigi. Leave it alone. It knows it cannot escape that way. Perhaps it is trying to show us something.*

"Yes, yes!" I told Ramoom, trying to point up and *ana* again. It was difficult to do at that moment, since I was clinging to the underside of a nearly horizontal surface. My hair kept falling into my eyes, and my arms were aching. I couldn't climb much longer without a rest. And was it even going to work? I could only communicate with Ramoom by answering yes or no questions. He might never understand what I was trying to tell him.

*You are wrong, Ramoom! It is going to kill itself. It has nothing to show us. It is running mindlessly.*

"No, no, no!" I shouted, loud enough for them to hear, at the same time trying to appear rational. But it's not easy to scream without sounding hysterical—especially when you're out of breath, hanging fifty feet in the air, and trying to negotiate around a non-euclidean object.

*Did you hear that? Their sound for the negative. It is denying what you say, Gigigi.*

"Yes, yes, yes!" I called as I reached an edge and a new face. This one slanted up and *ana* at something equivalent to a forty-five-degree angle. I hoisted myself up onto it, climbed a few feet, wedged in my hands and feet, and stretched out against it, giving my arms a chance to rest. *Kata* inside the cage, through layers of grid, Pete was turning in a circle, trying to find me. He was worried, but he was also furious—especially now that I was getting all the attention. In a minute he'd do something drastic to get it back. I started climbing again.

*But what could it be trying to tell us, Ramoom? I am afraid it will get hurt. Please, just let me—*

*Take one step closer to the cage and I will lock you outside again, repulsiveness!*

I wasn't looking at them, but I could sense his threatening gesture and her shrinking away, and I heard her whimper like a truck putting on the brakes. I hated Ramoom for the way he browbeat her, using her deformity against her, constantly threatening to leave and telling her that no one else could stand to live with her. Then why did he? Not out of kindness and self-sacrifice, I was sure of that. More likely he stayed because her appearance made her vulnerable and gave him power over her. He liked power, and maybe he had problems exerting it in the normal 4-space world. So he had to turn to a poor creature like Gigigi to make himself feel big.

And how much bigger would 3-space make him feel? To someone like Ramoom, it would be irresistible. He was exactly the worst kind of person to find out about 3-space. Though no one would be immune to the temptation of a universe to control. Even Gigigi, who was basically decent and kind, could turn out to be a menace.

That was when I wondered, for the first time, why no 4-space creature had ever stumbled on 3-space before. What had been preventing it all this time?

Then I reached the top of the cage and forgot that question. Everything would be decided in the next few minutes. And whether I lived through it or not was completely up to Omar.

# 18

There was quite a stiff breeze up here.

I clambered up onto the top of the cage and tried to get a good footing on the edge. It was like standing on a roof made out of chain-link fencing. I looked out across the room through the trinocs.

Like the cage, everything had too many edges and sides. There was a dirty cavern, like an entrance to a twisted subway tunnel, which must be a fireplace. Two draped plateaus loomed sideways in the distance, probably beds. Closer to the cage stood a curved-around table, with spherical dishes on it that somehow did not roll off, and multilayered angular structures that could have been books. Gigigi cowered behind the table, and Ramoom stood with his back against it, his four arms spread, protecting the cage.

A smaller table, with the maze on it, stood between Ramoom and the cage. That was good. It would prevent Ramoom from getting to me in time. I came as close as I dared to the edge of the roof and peered directly down forty feet into the maze. I could see into it, I could even see the pig thing, slobbering and snorting, battering at the wall with its tusks, still ravenous. That was good too.

For an instant, just out of curiosity, I pulled off the trinocs. The room dissolved into an abstract pattern of cross sectior.s, pyramids and boxes and spheres, eyeballs and nostrils shifting around wildly every time I moved my head—the inside of a kaleidoscope again. I slipped the trinocs back on. I couldn't put off what I had to do now.

I looked at Ramoom and pointed up and *ana,* the direction of the sky. "That is where we come from!" I told him. "That is the direction of our home. Yes, yes, yes!"

"Huh? What are you trying to do?" I heard Pete's little voice chirping from the cage.

"Yes, yes," I said, continuing to point in the direction of the sky. "That is our home. You cannot go there. But we can."

Ramoom peered at me, his mouth wrapping itself around his chin in a puzzled frown. *Little one is expressing the affirmative and pointing toward the sky. What can it mean?*

Brilliant Ramoom, always so clever when it was to our disadvantage, was turning out to be stupid now that I was depending on him to be smart. (And what about Omar? Would he be smart enough when the time came? But I pushed that worry away. It would paralyze me.)

"Home is that way!" I screamed, pointing and looking *ana* and up. Wind tore at my muddy sweatshirt. "Home. In that direction." I jumped for emphasis, and when I landed, my feet slipped out from under me on the grid. I landed, sliding on my rear end, and just managed to keep myself from flying off the edge of the roof by grabbing with my hands behind me. I felt my heart thudding in my neck as I got back to my feet.

*Ramoom, it is going to fall! Please, let me—*

He pushed her away, almost knocking her down. *Can't you see it is trying to tell me something? Only if it doesn't make itself clear very soon, then I will lock it up again and make them guide me, step-by-step, back to where they came from.*

"Yes, yes, that's it!" I shouted, dancing and pointing.

"No, no, no!" I heard Pete contradict me from below.

"Shut up and keep out of this!" I screamed at him.

"She's lying," he peeped at Ramoom. "No, no, no!"

If I kept yelling at Pete, it would only confuse things. All I could do was to keep saying yes and pointing up. But it had never occurred to me that Ramoom wouldn't get the point. If he didn't figure it out soon, we were out of luck.

*You mean you don't know what little one says, Ramoom?* Mixed in with Gigigi's worries about my safety, I detected a gleeful sprinkling of superiority, the satisfaction of scoring a point. *Whenever you mention where they come from, little one points toward sky and expresses the affirmative. It is obvious, Ramoom.* Giggles like an earthquake in a Venetian glassworks. *They fell from sky. Good luck finding the way there. Good luck finding other little ones.*

*Do not laugh, monstrosity, or I will rend your mouth so that you can never laugh again!* He turned to address me. *Is that it? You are telling me you come from the sky?*

"Yes, yes, yes!"

*And that all the other creatures like you . . . are somewhere up in the sky?*

"Yes, yes, yes!"

"No, no, no!" Pete contradicted.

*Wait! What is this? Other little one—the good, obedient, trustworthy little one—does not agree.*

Naturally Ramoom did not want to believe that we came from the sky or from any region that was inaccessible to him, which was the basic point I was trying to get across. His dislike of that idea was probably what had made him so slow to figure it out. And now that he finally had it, Pete—good, obedient, trustworthy Pete—was messing everything up.

"Stop it, Pete! You don't understand. Our only chance of living through this is if he believes me!"

"No! Our only chance of getting home is if he takes us there!"

*How can they disagree about such a thing? It makes no sense at all . . . unless one of them is lying, to hide the others from me.*

"Yes, yes, she is lying!"

"Are you there, Omar?" I said, preparing myself. "Be ready." Omar would have to stop us in seconds if Pete kept that up. I had to do this. I stepped to the very edge. I pointed up. "That is where we come from. I will prove it."

*Yes, Ramoom, one of them is lying—the one inside the cage. It is clear that they are creatures of the air. They are like delicate tufts of cloud, like sunlight. And remember how that little one went through the wall?* It almost seemed that Gigigi was on my side, that *she* wanted Ramoom to believe we came from somewhere "above." I didn't understand it, but I sure did appreciate it. *Could any creature of this earth go through a solid wall? No, Ramoom. They are from some sky realm that we cannot reach, that you must give up any hope of finding.*

"No, no, no! We are from nearby. You can so find it!"

"Yes, yes, yes!"

*But it is a very simple matter to test, Gigigi. We merely ask little one in cage to show us the way. Will you show us?*

I had to move. "I am going home. Watch me go!" I cried out. I bent my knees, swung my arms, and dived headfirst off the edge of the roof, aiming myself at the pig thing thirty feet below in the maze.

And at that moment, I saw the flaw in my plan.

# 19

The tusks rushed up at me more quickly than I had anticipated. I would land very close to the pig thing, which was looking up now. But I had little time to congratulate myself on my aim.

Everything happened very fast, the spiked walls zooming toward me, Pete's little voice fading away above me, the shock and alarm from Gigigi and Ramoom. My stomach seemed to be somewhere around my knees. Wind whistled past my face, my hair splayed out above my head. I sensed the movement of lumbering bodies, heard the heavy swish of fabric like great proscenium curtains sweeping together.

I had hoped that because Omar had saved me from the pig thing once before, he would save me this time too. But what

I had neglected to consider was that, according to Omar's rules, I was *supposed* to die. This time, he might just let it happen.

My life did not pass before my eyes. All that passed before my eyes was the pig thing, rapidly increasing in size, its eyes alert, its mouth open, squealing in hungry anticipation. I was close enough now to see the thick ropes of saliva dangling from its hairy maw.

"Omaaaar!" I wailed as the walls of the maze shot up around me.

And Omar, in the last second, did come through. The maze and the pig thing flattened and veered off to the side. Everything blurred and vanished as I was pulled away in that other unexpected direction.

I hit something soft and stopped abruptly. For a moment all I could do was lie there. Then I heard a familiar voice saying "Oh, Laura, *now* look what you've done!"

I sat up and looked around. I was in a very peculiar place indeed. But that seemed to be Omar, close beside me, holding both my hands.

And as I had suspected, he was not alone.

# 20

"*Why*, Laura?"

"Wait a minute, Omar. Let me get my bearings."

But if I'd had any hopes of getting adjusted to this place, I lost them in the next microsecond. We seemed to be hanging sideways on a cliff made out of doilies, endless lacy filigrees constantly flickering in and out of existence. There is no way to describe it. It was a total abstraction.

And was that really Omar? It took me a minute to be sure, since out here, wherever it was we were, he didn't only shrink to a line from the wrong angle, he also got squashed down into a little pink dot. I did recognize the opera-singing 4-space person. But as for the creature beside him—the thing so impossibly dense and complex that Gigigi and Ramoom were flat paper dolls in comparison—the look of that thing, even now, doesn't bear thinking about.

"Laura, answer me. Why did you jump? Now we'll just be in *more* trouble with the upper guardians. You don't know what I had to go through to save you the first time. They said I should let you die. And now you force me to bring you up *here*! No one's ever broken that law."

"But I had to, Omar. Listen." I tried to sound sure of myself. "It will only prove to Ramoom that we come from someplace he can't get to—someplace like this, maybe. That's why I did it."

"You don't know what you're talking about, Laura. You're not making any sense. Did you know I held them off as long as I could? They were supposed to kill you right away. I can't *believe* all the trouble you've—"

"Omar, I *do* know what I'm saying," I interrupted. "I was out there long enough to figure—"

But Omar didn't even stop. "—gotten me into. I'm ruined. After this, they'll—"

"—out a few things that even *you* might not realize. If you'd just shut up for a second and let me—"

"*OOOOOOOMMMMMARRRRRR. BEEEEEEEEEE QUIIIIIIET.*"

It was the incomprehensible one who had spoken. I could hear her voice in my ears and also feel it inside my head as well as inside my guts and my bones, vibrating through me as though I were sitting on the surface of a great bell when she spoke. It was a far more alien sensation than the voices of Gigigi and Ramoom—yet at the same time I was sure, as soon as I felt the voice, that the creature was female. She was situated around, inside and above a sort of bower or canopy, draped with things like pink ribbons and flounces and bows— anyway, I chose to believe they were ribbons, rather than entrails.

*"EXXXXXPLAINNNNNN YOURRRRRRSELFFFF, LAUAUAURRRRRRAAAA."*

It was not a voice to be disobeyed. I gulped, then blurted it out. "Well, see, I figured they didn't know about the different dimensions. When you took me through the wall, Omar, that tipped me off that you were watching from someplace. And they didn't understand it. They had no idea about going *up* into another dimension and crossing over a wall. So I thought if I kept telling them we were from *above* them, and then I jumped off, and you pulled me out here and I vanished, then they might get the idea they *couldn't* get to the place we came from."

"I can't believe you did that. That you *trusted* me that much," Omar said. I noticed how pale and nervous he was. And I realized that the reason he had been so angry at me was that he was scared. Scared of what had almost happened to me.

"I do trust you, Omar," I said, staring into the anterior chamber of his eye, his lens, his ciliary muscle, and his optic nerve. "I trust you more than anyone." Then I looked away, trying to get my thoughts organized. I was going to have to be pretty convincing if I was going to persuade the others to let me live.

*"GGGGGGOOOOOOO ONNNNNNNNNNNN."*

I wiped my forehead with my stiff, grimy sleeve. "Well, I thought if it looked to them like I flew away and vanished, they might get the idea we came from a *higher* space, instead of a lower one. They're pretty smart. A space they couldn't get to. Someplace like this . . . Like 5-space. . . . That's where we are, isn't it?" And I looked up and around at the creature, to see if I was right.

But I couldn't tell anything from looking at her. To me, even with the trinocs on, she was all cross sections. Four-dimensional cross sections. The burning scarlet eye rotating before me was a solid hypersphere, an eye within an eye within an eye, each with its own spherical iris and pupil. Spinning lazily behind and above the eyes hung a tuba-shaped organ, spreading out and opening into a yellow cavern festooned with twisting corkscrews of moist tissue. Part of a mouth? I didn't want to know, and looked quickly away.

"*YESSSSSSSSSS. YOUOUOUOUOU ARRRRRRRRE INNNNNNNN FIIIIIIIIIIIVE-SPAAAAAAAACE.*"

"But I thought . . . she wasn't supposed to know about that!" Omar burst out, confused.

*She already knows it, Omar.* That must be the 4-space guy; his thoughts reminded me of Gigigi and Ramoom. *She knows a great deal, it seems. She is indeed intelligent, as you told us. Let her continue.*

"Thanks," I said, feeling like a witness being cross-examined. The 4-space guy was relatively easy for me to comprehend now, even though out here in 5-space I could see inside him, too. He *looked* like a character from an opera, a shaggy, hulking creature in garments of leather and metal, with things that might be weapons dangling from his belt. Like Gigigi and Ramoom, he had four arms, four legs, and three eyes. "Anyway," I went on, "I guess that's most of it. I knew that you would have to . . . to kill us, before we gave anything away about 3-space. I can understand it, in a way. But I also wanted to try to prevent it if I could. Like I said, if I could make them think we came from *above* them, maybe that would be *better* than killing us. If we just died, Ramoom would still go around trying to find 3-space. But if they thought there was no way they could ever *get* to 3-space, then Ramoom would have to give up. And if they thought we could just disappear like that, then they wouldn't try to capture anybody else."

"Well, maybe," Omar said doubtfully. "But we're not supposed to do that—that was another rule I broke to save you from pain—because then they might figure out about—"

"About 5-space?" I interrupted. "So what if they did? They

146 |

can't *get* to 5-space on their own, like they can get to 3-space. They can't *interfere* with 5-space, like they can with 3-space. 5-space is safe from the dimension below it. So why shouldn't they know about it? Isn't that better than us dying?"

"Except that it's breaking the first rule. The most important rule: Preserve Ignorance."

*"PRRRRRRRRESERVVVVVVE IGNNNNNNNNO-RRRRRRRRANCE,"* intoned the 5-space lady, and the lace and ribbons fluttered as all three of them sighed deeply.

"But there's one other thing," I said, suddenly remembering. "Gigigi and Ramoom might not be so ignorant about 5-space. You didn't notice, but I did. Gigigi is reversed."

"What are you talking about?"

I turned back to the 4-space guy. "How come *you* didn't notice? Gigigi's middle eye is *kata* from the other two. And her nose is *ana* from the eyes. Didn't you see that?"

*Watching from up here, it is easy not to notice reversal.* His thoughts were puzzled. *Are you sure?*

"Absolutely. They talk about it all the time. And I learned to see really well with these things. I had to. Her being reversed can only mean one thing, right? That somehow, sometime, she got pulled up here into 5-space and flipped over."

*"UNNNHHHHHEARDDDDD OOOFFFFFF!"* Even the deep, bell-like tones had taken on a tremulous quality.

I didn't like contradicting her, but I had one final point to make, and since I was arguing for my life, I didn't hesitate. "Well, it *must* have happened to her, and it must have been horrifying. And I thought, if we could make them connect *us* with that experience, then that would scare them away from meddling with any other dimensions for good. Being reversed is a lot more disfiguring to them than to us. And I think there's one more thing you could do, a good deed, that would *totally* protect 3-space from them, forever. If you rescue Pete, then you could just . . . Uh oh! Pete! What's he doing down there?

What's he telling them?" No matter how convincing I was, if Pete gave anything away, we were done for.

Omar shrank down to a pink dot. The 4-space guy flattened to a furry line. A grayish, puckering, tentacled thing leapt from the lady's hyperspherical eyes.

"Hey, come on, show me where to look," I pleaded. "I want to see too!"

Something that did not feel like Omar—I forced myself not to dwell on what exactly it might be—reached inside my face and pointed me very carefully in a specific direction. (I was glad the lady was careful about it, because it suddenly occurred to me that in 5-space I could easily get turned inside out.) I looked *kata,* above me, and another way that I had no name for.

It was like staring down from the top of an impossibly high skyscraper again. Yet at the same time I seemed to be underneath, or inside, the maze. Below the tilting crenellated walls and ramps hung the cage, a pointed, starlike object with a pink flatworm in one corner that had to be Pete.

Then Ramoom's six-fingered hand pulled Pete out of the cage and dangled him by his feet. *Tell me the truth! Help me find your friend. Or you go back inside the maze!*

"No, no, no!" chirped Pete, little threads filling up with blood inside his paper-doll face.

*Leave it alone, Ramoom!* Gigigi pleaded. *The other one has escaped. It has gone home.*

"Yes, yes, yes!" Pete screamed. "She went home, into the sky!"

"Omar, did you hear that?" I whispered. "Pete's going along with me now."

*No. You are lying to me!* Ramoom shook him. *Did it really go home?*

"Yes, yes, yes!" Pete insisted.

Ramoom flipped Pete up into the deeply furrowed palm of

his hand and held him up to his eyes. I could see right into Ramoom's hand, where the bones branched out in all directions like pale trees intertwined with pulsing serpents. *Listen carefully. You are the one I trusted,* Ramoom told him. *We will make a bargain. I will forget the other one. I will take you home and leave you there. All you have to do is guide me to the spot, and you will be safe at home forever. Ramoom will promise.* He smiled, his face splitting open as rows of crumbling battlements jutted out of it.

"Well, uh . . . I don't know," Pete mumbled, twisting his head away from Ramoom's face.

*And if you refuse to show me,* Ramoom thought at him, the rictus of his smile still stretched across his head, *then you will go back inside the box with our hungry friend.*

*No, Ramoom, I will not let you. Fly away, little one. Fly away!*

*I will tear you apart, deformity!* Ramoom swatted her away with two of his other hands, and she stumbled to the floor. *You have much to gain if you accept my offer and everything to lose it you don't,* he coaxed, his grin remaining fixed in place.

"Laura? Can you hear me?" Pete whimpered. "What happened to you? Where are you? Can you take me there too?"

"Omar, let me talk to him. Let me tell him he can come here!" I whispered. "Then he won't go along with Ramoom."

"No," Omar said flatly. "It's bad enough that we brought you up here. There's no chance they'll take him too."

"But you can't let him die!"

*"IIIIII AMMMMMM SORRRRRRRRY, LAUAUAU-RRRRRA. HHHHHHHEEEEEE MMMMMAYYYYYY NNNNNNOTTTTT COMMMMMME HERRRRRRE."*

*We understand your thinking, Laura. It was the 4-space guy. But you do not understand the enormity and danger of breaking so many laws. It is not only up to the three of us. Others, with more power, will know. We have already endangered ourselves by bringing you here.*

I could feel that he would not budge. "But if you just leave him there he'll *have* to give in and show Ramoom where we—"

*We will stop him before he does.*

*Your time is up, my little about-to-be-eaten friend.* Ramoom dangled Pete over the maze again. *Promise to show me now.*

"Laura, I can't wait any longer!" Pete wailed.

At that moment I remembered, again, the part of my plan I hadn't had a chance to tell them. "Wait, listen!" I said. "You can still save him. You don't have to bring him here. And you can do a good deed too. All you have to do is this."

# 21

It was the 5-space lady who did it—and who decided to break one more rule and let us live.

She seemed to like me for some reason. She also liked my plan. I wonder how much it had to do with the fact that the three of us—she and Gigigi and I—were all females.

At the time I was disappointed that she didn't let me watch the actual mechanics of it. That was probably wise of her. It must have been a pretty grisly sight. Still, even now I often find myself speculating about what exactly the transformation looked like.

The last thing she said to me, before sending us off, was *"LAURRRRAA, SSSSOOOOO DDDDDDELICATE*

*ANNNND DDDDDDAINNNTEEEE. HHHHOWWW
DDDDO IIIIIII LOOOOOOOOK TOOOO ONNNNNE
FRROMMMMM THREEEE-SSSSSPACE?"*

I took a final look at her hyperspherical eyes, now enmeshed in a kind of gooey web made out of things like beef tongues. "Well, you're the most . . . uh, fascinating and charismatic woman I've ever met" was what I managed to come up with, not daring to lie to her.

She seemed satisfied. *"THTHTHANKKKK YYYOUOU MMMMMMMY DDDDDDDDEARRRRRR,"* she rumbled as we fell into 4-space.

She did the thing while Omar and I and the 4-space guy— or guardian, as Omar called him—waited outside Gigigi and Ramoom's cottage. I listened hard, but all I heard from inside were a couple of gasps and thumps. Then she must have given the 4-space guardian a signal. He hurried inside to find Pete and get him out of there. I let him take care of that. He didn't need my help. And I was desperately curious about Gigigi and Ramoom.

I found them quickly, from the vantage point of the guardian's shoulder. The 5-space lady had done a neat job, depositing each of them on a bed. They both lay facedown, whimpering and groaning, and I could feel how disoriented they were— though Ramoom seemed to be worse off than Gigigi.

*Ohhhhh . . . What was that? Gigigi, I have just had the most terrible experience. I think it was an attack of some kind.*

*I felt it too, Ramoom. Only . . . it seems to me that long, long ago, I felt something like it, once before.*

*You lie, repulsiveness! Whenever anything happens to me, you claim it happens to you as well. You always demand attention for yourself.*

*Oh, Ramoom! It happened to us both. And I tell you, I have felt something like it before. . . .*

Then Pete was plopped down onto the shoulder beside me, sagging weakly against me. The guardian quickly left the cottage and started across the clearing.

"Please, can't we just wait a minute?" I said. "I know they mustn't see us, but you could hide behind a tree if they come out. I've just *got* to hear it when they realize what happened."

*Well . . . only for a moment.* He crouched down just outside the clearing. He seemed to have developed some respect for me.

*It is passing from me, Ramoom. I feel somewhat better. Would you like me to bring you something to drink, to soothe you?*

*Ohhhh, yessss. I am still so dizzy. Clearly it hit me worse than you, whatever you may claim. But first, make sure the little one has not escaped. Be quick about it!*

*I'm sorry, Ramoom.* I felt her sadness. *It is gone. It is probably just as well. I think that is part of what happened to us.*

*What? You ugly imbecile! How could you let it—?*

*Ramoom! Oh, no, Ramoom! What has happened to your face?*

Pete stirred against me. "Laura? Where are we? Did we get away from—?"

"Shhh, Pete! I've got to hear this!"

*Stop your babbling, twisted one! You cannot distract me from the fact that you have let the little one escape. I know your tricks.*

*But, Ramoom, your face!* A moment of confusion. Then amazement and an intense flood of joy. *But I can feel . . . I think something has happened to me as well. Look at me, Ramoom!*

*Oh, stop your idiot ravings, twisted—* Then from Ramoom a burst of shock.

*Twisted, Ramoom? Twisted what, my friend? Come here, to the looking glass . . . if you dare.* Giggles, like a hundred creaking doors opening at once, like blocks of ice crashing together in a suddenly thawing river.

"I don't get it, Laura. What are they—"

"*Shhh!*"

*No! It is not possible! What have you done to meeeeee?* Horror, a moment of impotent rage, dwindling away into sniveling self-pity.

*I, Ramoom? I have done nothing. It must have been a warning, from the little ones in the sky. Perhaps if you had not been so cruel, the warning would have been less brutal for you.*

The guardian stood up and began moving away through the forest. *We have heard enough now, I think.*

I strained to catch the last of their conversation. *But what will I do now? I can never go out in the world again!* His thoughts were fading. *I do not dare to leave this cottage. How could this happen to me? It is not fair.*

*Not fair, Ramoom? But perhaps I should call you twisted one now. And speaking of the rest of the world . . . perhaps it is time for me to take a look at it.*

*No, Gigigi. Please! Do not leave me. You must not leave me. Please stay! You must promise. . . .*

The guardian began to sing. "Tra la-la la! Tra la-la la!" his voice boomed out, and I could feel the vocal cords in his throat vibrating near me. His shoulder muscles bunched up beneath me as his arms began to swing, a not unpleasant rolling sensation that reminded me of the time, years ago at a children's zoo, when I had ridden on an elephant.

"I don't get it, Laura. What were they talking about? How did we get out of there?"

"Pete, I just want to tell you. I saw how you held out back there, how you didn't give in to Ramoom." I almost felt a little choked up now at what I had to do and how well Pete had finally come through in the end. "You were great, Pete. And now it's almost over."

"I'm glad I meet with your approval, Laura," he said sarcastically. "But that doesn't explain how we got out of there. How did you do that disappearing act? And what's this . . . thing we're riding on? Where are we going?"

He had no way of knowing that we were riding on a friendly guardian, like a character out of a fairy tale, because he wasn't wearing trinocs. Remembering them, I quickly took the trinocs off and slipped them into my pocket—in case the guardian wouldn't want me to keep them. At the same time, I took several packets of ketchup out of my other pocket. I hoped Pete wasn't going to be stubborn and pigheaded now.

"Laura, will you answer me! What is *happening*? Where are we going?"

"It's almost over, Pete. In a few minutes you'll wake up in your own room. In a day or so, you'll forget you ever had this bad dream."

"Don't feed me that! Just tell me what's going on!"

"Relax, Pete. Look around. It's your last chance to see any of this."

I couldn't relax yet; I was too worried about what was going to happen to Pete. But I was glad to be going home, glad of the guardian's protection. We moved swiftly through the darkening forest, tendrils and leaves, branches and bright blossoms expanding and contracting around us. I could hear the vast sighing of the trees, an accompaniment to the guardian's song, and distant birds shrieking in the twilight. *Ana* and above us sailed the blue and green moons, shrinking and blowing up like balloons. Only yesterday all this had seemed nightmarish to me. Now I saw how beautiful it was. Someday I would be back.

Ahead of us loomed a dark wall of trees, dense and thick and unbroken. The guardian stopped beside it. The time had come to deal with Pete.

I tore open a couple of packets. I couldn't tell if the writing was reversed, but I had to hope that some of the ketchup was.

They had agreed to let Pete live—but only if I could convince him that none of this had really happened. Getting him stoned on ketchup was the only way to accomplish that. "Here, have some ketchup, Pete," I said, trying to sound casual. "Remember how much you liked it before?"

"Ketchup? *Now* what's the matter with you? What happened to Gigigi and Ramoom? Are we really going home?"

"Yes, we're going home—*if* you eat the ketchup. It's what got you into this trip, and it's the only thing that'll take you out of it."

"Lay off with the ketchup! Stop being so bossy and give me some answers. I deserve to know!"

It was true; he did deserve to know. But it was also true that the guardian wouldn't let him out of here alive unless he ate the ketchup. Preserving ignorance was terribly important to the people in control. "I'm telling you, Pete. This was all a gigantic hallucination. This ketchup is the only thing that'll stop it. If you don't eat it, we'll *both* be here forever. And I want to go home."

"Stop it, Laura! How stupid do you think I am? Tell me the truth!"

I wished that I could. Pete had ended up behaving decently, and his reward was to be deceived. I couldn't even tell him that he would die if he didn't do what I asked. He wasn't supposed to know that either. "Trust me, Pete," I said, hoping he wouldn't notice how unsure I sounded. "The only way you'll ever get out of this fantasy is if you take this antidote. After that, I'll answer anything you want. Anyway, why *not*? Please, Pete!"

"Just like a girl, always have to have your own way," he muttered. "Give it to me." He squeezed two packets down his throat.

"Here, Pete. Two more, okay?"

He rolled his eyes and groaned. "You didn't say I had to eat *four* of . . ." Then he grinned crookedly.

He was feeling it! "Come on, Pete," I said, so relieved I wanted to kiss the plastic containers. "Doesn't it taste great?"

"Sure does. Gimme some more." He gulped down the rest. Then he looked around, swaying beside me. "*Love* those two moons, don't you? Great effect. They look so real. Make me feel twice as romantic." He slipped his arm around me.

"Ready to go," I said hastily into the guardian's ear, an oval curlicue of flesh hanging beside my head.

The guardian bent over, and using all four hands, he pushed the wall of foliage apart. He whispered something I didn't quite pick up. He stepped through.

We stood on the shore of a lake. Not a 3-space lake, with a flat surface. A 4-space lake, its surface spherical, domed, glowing from within, tilting away from us, curving around in the *ana* and *kata* directions. And so, too, did the shoreline curve, undulating *ana* and *kata* to enclose this strange body of water—except that it was not water. It was space. Our space. The three-dimensional surface of a hypersphere.

I almost put on the trinocs. That would be the only way to comprehend the intersection of the two spaces, to see clearly how our entire universe could be surrounded by a 4-space jungle. But I did not dare. I wanted to keep the trinocs, and the guardian seemed to have forgotten that I had them. I was pretty sure he'd take them away if he saw them now. This time I had to be content with a partial view. Later I might have another chance to see it better.

The guardian peered down at the surface of the lake, then moved along a few steps. He was familiar with the shoreline; he had taken a path that led almost directly to the right spot. Here, within the lake, swam pink and blue clouds, trees, houses and roads.

"Hey, Laura, it's only a cartoon," Pete murmured, nuzzling my ear. "And you know what you're *supposed* to do at a drive-in movie. . . ."

Maybe four packets had been a little too much ketchup. But I refused to worry about that now. I wanted to see as much as I could. Around the edges of the lake marched other figures. I couldn't see them clearly now, but the shapes of the nearer ones looked similar to the friend who had given us a lift here. Other guardians, constantly patrolling and protecting our universe? And were they the reason that 4-space people didn't stumble across it?

I turned quickly away from them, my eyes sweeping across the surface, hoping, in the few seconds I had left, to get a glimpse of another part of the universe. A spot that was only a few steps away on the twisting shoreline could easily be hundreds of light-years distant to the creatures trapped on the surface. My eyes raked across the blackness of empty space, blinked against the fiery blaze of a star, then focused in on a world of barren pockmarked mountains and ice, where nothing moved. Not the kind of world I was hoping to see. I wanted a world with life on it, with civilizations. But such worlds must be rare. My eyes flashed away again.

"C'mon, Laura. Warm up a li'l," Pete whispered drowsily.

*Yes, he seems sufficiently inebriated,* the guardian thought at me, and pulled him away. Pete was safe now. The guardian lifted me with another hand and stretched it out over the surface of the lake. The surface swelled and magnified, surrounding me. I saw, out of the corner of my eye, the guardian dropping Pete into his house. Then there was my street, and my house, the inside and outside of every room. The place I had been so desperate to get back to when we had first fallen out into 4-space.

But now I wanted something else. My mind was racing with adrenaline. I knew I had to be careful, that if I fell down in the wrong place I could end up millions of miles from home, in the middle of an ocean or empty space. But I also, somehow, knew exactly what to do. Omar, in one of the guardian's other hands, was quite close to me. And when the guardian started to drop Omar, I lunged out of his hand and grabbed Omar around the waist.

And fell with Omar into a place very close to home, but where I had never been before: the inside of old Mr. Campanelli's house.

"Laura, what are you doing? Let go of me! Let goooo. . . ."

We landed on the dark basement floor. Around us hung pipes and spiderwebs, a furnace, a lot of dust, a wet moldy smell.

"Laura, don't look!" Omar screamed. "You're not supposed to be here! You're not supposed to know!"

"Too late, Omar."

I stared down, amazed, at the beautiful glittering thing, full of movement and life. I had not, until this very instant, realized that it existed.

Yet now that I saw it, I knew exactly what it was.

# 22

"Every point in a dimension $N$ is accessible from—and vulnerable to—the dimension $N + 1$."

That's the universal law of the dimensions, and the reason why all the guardians are necessary—from the guardians of 1-space, 2-space, 3-space and 4-space, all the way up to the guardians of $\infty - 1 =$ space.

Infinite-dimensional space—sometimes known as Hilbert space—is the only exception. They don't need any guardians all the way up there. That's because there isn't anybody they need to be guarded from. They're at the very top of the pile.

Meanwhile, down here at the bottom . . .

Omar started toward me as if to push me away from the glittering thing, to cover my eyes. But an instant later he realized that it was, as I had said, too late. He slumped down onto his knees and put his hands over his own eyes.

And I gazed down at the 2-space universe. "No wonder Mr. Campanelli is so afraid of the highway commission," I murmured.

2-space was big. And it wasn't a flat plane; it seemed to be a bubble. We weren't really in a basement, but in a cave that extended into dimness as far as I could see. The only light came from the gleaming shape, like some huge dirigible, that curved away into the distance. The 2-space universe was the flat surface of this balloon—just as our universe is the three-dimensional surface of a 4-space hypershape.

I could clearly see the creatures moving around on the balloon, the living "paper dolls"—though they didn't look like any paper dolls I had ever imagined. They didn't stare up from the surface like paper dolls, but they weren't exactly profiles either. When they wanted to change direction or look the other way, they couldn't turn around in three dimensions, as we do. Instead, they had to turn *over* on the flat surface. That made their anatomy, from my point of view, very peculiar indeed.

The basic shape of their bodies was something like a fat capital *B*. They had two limbs coming out of the top of the *B*, and two limbs coming out of the bottom. To my surprise, they also had two eyes, each one at the edge of one of the rounded parts of the *B*. The indentation between the eyes was the mouth. When they wanted to change direction or look the other way, they bent over in the middle, sort of like a person doing a cartwheel, so that the top limbs became the bottom limbs and vice versa. When the limbs were on the bottom, they functioned as legs and feet, and when they were on the top, they functioned as arms and hands. Actually, they only looked like *B*'s when they were moving from left to right. When they moved from right to left they looked like ꓭ's.

Something was puzzling me, and since Omar was standing

beside me now, I asked him about it. "But Omar, they're not like that profile you showed me with the big nose pointing one way. So if I flipped one of them over in 3-space, how would the others know he was reversed?"

"No, Laura! Don't do it!" he cried, reaching for my hands.

"Come on, Omar, I wouldn't do that," I promised, shaking him off. "But how *would* they notice if one of them got reversed?"

He was shaken and upset that I had discovered the existence of 2-space, but that didn't mean he wasn't glad to show off his superior knowledge. "First of all, did anybody instantly notice when *I* was reversed, or when you were?" he asked me. "Did your *mother* even notice?"

"Oh . . . that's right, I guess they didn't."

"All right. But, on the other hand, these people *would* notice. Take a closer look. Can't you see the nose, and the ear?"

I studied them more carefully. And I saw that the flat side of the *B* wasn't really flat. There was a little triangular bump opposite one of the eyes and a little round bump opposite the other eye.

"When they're going from left to right, the nose is on the top and the ear is on the bottom," Omar said. "And when they're going from right to left, the nose is on the bottom and the ear is on the top. So if one of them *did* get flipped over in 3-space, the nose and the ear would be reversed. Just like with Gigigi and Ramoom, he would seem like some kind of horrible, unnatural monster to the others. They would do terrible things to him. That's exactly the kind of thing we're here to prevent."

"What do you mean *we?*"

He sighed. "Look around the edges, Laura."

I looked. And I saw people, like Omar, moving around the periphery of the gleaming bubble—some below it, some on catwalks above it. People patrolling it just as I had seen the guardians patrolling the 4-space lake that was our universe.

"Guardians," I breathed.

Omar nodded. "Other guardians . . . like me," he said.

"*You're* a guardian, Omar?"

"Well, an apprentice," he admitted. "I came here to learn, and to replace Mr. Campanelli when he gets too old."

"So that's what all your 'duties' were, and why you'd never let me in here," I said. And at that moment I began to understand the universal law of dimensions I quoted at the beginning of this chapter, and part of what it implies. But I still didn't understand everything. "2-space is vulnerable to 3-space, just as 3-space is vulnerable to 4-space," I said. "So you're protecting *them* from other 3-space people, and the 4-space guardians are protecting *us* from other 4-space people."

"Now do you see why it *has* to be a secret? Why it's so important to preserve ignorance?" Omar said. "What if somebody like Pete found out about 2-space? The guardians are some protection, but not really enough. Pete could sneak past them and cause trouble in 2-space, like Ramoom could do in 3-space, if he knew where it was. The guardians don't even want *you* to know about 2-space."

"But wait a minute, Omar. Okay, so there's 2-space and 3-space and 4-space and 5-space. But why should it stop there? Why shouldn't there be 6-space and 7-space and 8-space and . . . and every other number of space too?"

"Don't, Laura," Omar said, backing away, sounding scared again. "Can't you just leave it at what you already know? Can't you just for once stop prying, stop finding out more than you're supposed to?"

He was still trying to hide something from me, and that's what gave the whole thing away. "There *are* all those other dimensions, Omar, aren't there?" I demanded. "There's one dimension on top of another, all the way up to . . . to wherever it stops. And each one has to be protected from the one above it, because each one is vulnerable to the one above it. It's like a balancing act in a circus or . . . kind of a chain reaction. If the one on the bottom falls down, then all the other ones do too. So we protect 2-space to be sure 4-space protects us. And 4-space protects us to be sure 5-space protects them— *She* was a guardian too, the 5-space lady, wasn't she? And she protects 4-space to be sure 6-space protects *her*. And on and on. Isn't that right, Omar?"

"Stop it, Laura, stop it," he moaned. "Don't even say it out loud. Only the guardians are supposed to know. If the rest of the world found out about it, if the structure broke down, then . . . It's too terrible to imagine."

"But *you're* the one who gave the whole thing away, Omar," I pointed out. "Sure, I made the mistake of going out there with Pete. But I didn't understand much then. You *did* understand, and you told me anyway. You're the one who betrayed your sacred trust."

"But I was just so lonely, Laura," he said, touching my arm. "I thought it was the only way you would ever be my friend. I didn't think it would turn out like this. You . . . might have done the same thing."

"If I knew as much as you did? I don't know, Omar," I said. "But you know what? Just because the kids at school were unfriendly to you *doesn't* automatically mean you're a good person."

"Please, Laura, don't be so quick to accuse me." He squeezed my hand. "You don't know what I had to go through to get them to take you up into 5-space. And you don't seem to realize how unusual it is that they might let you go on knowing about it."

"Oh. Well, uh, thanks for doing that, Omar." I returned the pressure of his hand. "But *she'll* be on my side, won't she? The

5-space lady. She trusted me. And she's . . ." It was hard to think of the right word for her. "She's . . . *big*, and important."

"Don't make the mistake of thinking she's like God," Omar warned me. "You never saw the 6-space one, bigger than her. They're all going to have to decide what to do about you."

"But *when*, Omar?" I said, frightened now, still gripping his hand. Soft and moist as it was, it was a lot more comforting than Pete's hand had been. Omar had certainly demonstrated that I could trust him. Maybe that was why his hand felt so good.

"It's going to be soon, Laura. Look. Here comes Mr. Campanelli."

A figure leaning on a cane was approaching us, a dark silhouette against the radiant bubble of 2-space.

All that was years ago. Now I am a neurosurgeon.

Not to mention, a gastrointestinal surgeon, a cardiovascular surgeon, an orthopedic surgeon, and any other kind of surgeon you might want to name. I perform wonders. I make superficial incisions only to protect my secret. I've saved the lives of people who couldn't be helped in any other way.

The guardians did decide in my favor, largely because of the testimony of the 5-space lady (whose name, in translation, is the rough equivalent of Grace). But my knowledge and continued access to 4-space were allowed only if I agreed to certain specific conditions.

And in fact, despite my initial doubts, Omar has turned out to be as satisfactory a husband as anyone could wish. We are quite devoted to one another. Each of us is committed to a demanding career, and we often do not see one another for days at a time. But that only makes the time we have together all the more special. He is as fascinated to hear about what goes on inside my patients as I am to learn about the latest developments in 2-space. The secret and the responsibility that we share only strengthens our bond from year to year. And I would also like to say that although Omar is still shorter than I, he did turn out to be an attractive enough adult in an exotic sort of way, in my opinion anyway. Getting his tooth replaced helped a lot. We are very happy.

As for Pete, he managed to make me as unpopular as Omar. The stories he told about the weird drugs I gave him didn't damage my reputation. It was what he said about how cold and unapproachable and just plain peculiar I was that did the trick. But being an outsider didn't bother me as much as I might have expected. More than anything else, I was relieved that my plan had worked and Pete's ignorance—and life—were preserved. Not being popular was a trivial sacrifice to make considering the larger issues at stake.

And those issues are very large indeed. The balance between the dimensions turns out to be a great deal more delicate than I realized at first. One way to think of it is to imagine a series of balls balanced on top of one another, each one larger than the one supporting it, and the one at the bottom, holding up all the rest, the smallest of them all. One little nudge, especially down here in the lower dimensions, would upset the entire pile. The result would be a cataclysm so total that one can barely begin to comprehend it.

My parents, of course, are thrilled to have Omar and me living right next door to them in the house that used to belong to old Mr. Campanelli. We visit them often enough to compensate for the fact that, because of Omar's top secret government work (they believe), they can never enter our house. And they dote on Omar, Jr., who is already being prepared to take over his father's business.

When I glance in the mirror these days, I note without regret the touches of gray in my closely cropped hair, the tiny lines beginning to form at the edges of my lips and eyes. My life has turned out to be so spectacularly rewarding that even now, at times, I am amazed by my good fortune. Along with everything else, it is endlessly fascinating to continue to learn more about the various dimensions. For instance, why is 4-space so primitive, like the world in some of our ancient folktales? Advanced technology, it seems, only develops in the uneven dimensions. It amuses me no end to try to imagine what the advanced technology of one-dimensional space might be like.

About the only thing bothering me at the moment, in fact, is the dogged persistence of the state highway commission, which has still not given up the ridiculous notion of tearing down this block to build an interchange. Mr. Campanelli fought them for years, and we are continuing the fight. Unfortunately, we are now the only family still holding out against them, which weakens our position considerably. We cannot, of course, divulge our secret to the federal government, as crucial as that secret is to the security of the planet. Politicians would certainly wreak havoc upon the dimensional balance if they ever found out about it. The only solution now is the drastic one of appealing for intervention from the higher-dimensional guardians. Omar must do it soon. I have reason to suspect that the state highway commission is on the verge of resorting to unscrupulous, if not illegal, tactics.

And now the time has come for me to destroy this notebook. I have written this account not to preserve it on paper, but only to engrave these events on my own memory. It is the one secret I've kept from Omar. If he knew of its existence, he would be appalled, justifiably, at the risk I have taken in writing it.

What would happen if it ever fell into the hands of a publisher? I shudder to think.